WELL NOW, MY PRETTY . . .

For years, Serge Maisky had dreamed of the Big Steal. What better place, he decided, than the Paradise City Casino, where the richest gamblers in the world fought battles on the turn of a card? There he would be able to lay his hands on vast sums of money.

Here is the story of the Casino robbery written with the swift, sure efficiency that has put James Hadley Chase in the top echelon of thriller writers.

You will be hooked until the last page.

Also by James Hadley Chase

THE FLESH OF THE ORCHID
NO ORCHIDS FOR MISS BLANDISH
DO ME A FAVOUR—DROP DEAD
TRUSTED LIKE THE FOX
THIS IS FOR REAL
THE WAY THE COOKIE CRUMBLES
THE JOKER IN THE PACK
COME EASY, GO EASY
BELIEVED VIOLENT
THE FAST BUCK
BELIEVE THIS, YOU'LL BELIEVE ANYTHING
GOLDFISH HAVE NO HIDING PLACE
MAKE THE CORPSE WALK

and published by Corgi Books

Well Now, My Pretty . . .

James Hadley Chase

CORGI BOOKS

WELL NOW, MY PRETTY . . .

A CORGI BOOK 0 552 11558 4

Originally published in Great Britain by Robert Hale Limited

PRINTING HISTORY
Robert Hale edition published 1967
Corgi edition published 1980
Corgi edition reissued 1985

This book is set in Bembo 10 on 11 pt.

Corgi Books are published by Transworld Publishers Ltd., Century House, 61-63 Uxbridge Road, Ealing, London W5 5SA, in Australia by Transworld Publishers (Aust.) Pty. Ltd., 26 Harley Crescent, Condell Park, NSW 2200, and in New Zealand by Transworld Publishers (N.Z.) Ltd., Cnr. Moselle and Waipareira Avenues, Henderson, Auckland.

Made and printed in Great Britain by
Hunt Barnard Printing Ltd., Aylesbury, Bucks.

one

ONE OF the major attractions of Paradise City was the Aquarium. He had asked her to meet him by the Dolphin pool at four-thirty p.m. and she thought it was a pretty crummy place for a rendezvous. She hated mixing with the tourists who made Paradise City at this time completely unbearable.

During the third week of February when it was hot, but not too hot, it was the fashionable time for the Texans, the New Yorkers, as well as the South Americans, to come in a never-ending stream of overpoweringly rich vulgarity. Between the hours of four and five, after the siesta, and when there was nothing much to do until the Casino opened, crowds of tourists visited the cool, dimly lit caves that housed the most spectacular aquarium in the world.

She moved through the crowds, her green eyes restless and uneasy, her small body shrinking a little inside her simple cotton frock, as she made contact with the fat and the old, the raddled and the wrinkled who screamed, yelled, pushed and jostled to gape at the tropical fish that gaped back at them with equal incredulity.

Could she ever hope to find him here? she wondered, suddenly angry that he should have suggested such a meeting place. She felt hot fingers cup one of her buttocks and squeeze. She jerked forward, not looking over her shoulder. This was something she had grown accustomed to. The old and the too rich were prone to bottom pinching. She had long ceased to care. It was a hazard she accepted in return for a neat, well-proportioned body and an attractive face . . . you can't have it both ways, she had often told herself. You were either plain and non-sexy or you had bruises. She preferred the bruises.

She made her way towards the Dolphin pool, aware that her heart was thumping, aware too of a sick feeling of fear. As she walked, her eyes anxiously scanned every face that appeared out of the dim light, praying she would meet no one she knew or who knew who she was. But as the milling noisy crowd surrounded her, pushing, laughing and yelling at each other, she began to realise that his choice of a meeting place was clever. None of her friends, no one from the Casino, would dream of coming here to be jostled by this sweating, vulgar crowd of tourists, anxious only to kill an hour or so.

She edged her way into the big cave that housed the dolphins. Here, the crowd was dense. She could hear the big creatures splashing in the water as they dived for fish thrown to them. There was a dank smell in the cave, mixed with the smell of expensive perfume and body sweat; the noise of the crowd as it enjoyed itself, beat against her eardrums, making her cringe.

Then she saw him.

He came out of the crowd with his gentle smile, his white panama hat in his hand, his tropical cream-coloured suit immaculate, a blood-red carnation in his buttonhole. He was small and slightly built: a man in his early sixties, with a lean brown face, grey eyes and a thin mouth that was constantly smiling. His thinning blond hair was white at the temples and his nose was the beak of a hawk: a man she now distrusted, who she was learning to fear, but who attracted her with the pull of an electro-magnet to steel.

"Well now, my pretty . . ." he said, pausing before her. "So we meet again."

His voice was soft, but clear. She had never had any difficulty in hearing what he said no matter where they had met, even against the noisiest of backgrounds. This was always his greeting, "Well now, my pretty . . ." She knew it was as insincere as an alcoholic's promise but, like the bottom pinching, she had ceased to care.

When they had first met, he had told her his name was Franklin Ludovick. He had been born in Prague, and was a free-lance journalist. He had come to Paradise City to write an important profile on the Casino. This was not surprising. Many journalists had come to write about the Casino. It was the top glamour spot of Florida. At this period of the high season, a million dollars could, every night, cross the green-baized tables, more often the croupiers' way than the punters . . . but who cared?

Ludovick had approached her one afternoon while she was sun bathing on the beach. His harmless, kindly manner, his deference to her youth and his smile captivated her. He had explained that he knew she worked at the Casino. He gave her an embossed card, bearing his name with the magic *New Yorker* magazine added as his address and his reference. He explained that he was looking for inside information about the Casino. He sat at her feet on the soft sand, his panama hat resting almost on the bridge of his beaky nose as he talked. He told her he had had an interview with Harry Lewis, the manager of the Casino. His face screwed up in a comical grimace of despair. What a man! How secretive! If he had to rely on Harry Lewis's information, he would never produce anything to satisfy the *New Yorker*'s tremendously high standards. He felt he could approach her. She worked in the Casino's vault with a number of other girls. This, he had found out. He looked up at her, his grey eyes mischievous. Well then, my pretty . . . how often had she heard him use this phrase that she had come to fear and to distrust? Suppose you tell me what I want to know and I, in my turn, will pay you for the information? What shall we say? The *New Yorker* is a rich magazine. Five hundred dollars? How about five hundred dollars?

She had caught her breath. *Five hundred dollars!* She was hoping desperately to get married. Terry, her boy-friend, was still a student. They had both agreed that if they could only raise five hundred dollars, they could take a chance and get married, and at least have a one room walk-up . . . but how to get five hundred dollars? And here, now, was this harmless little man actually offering her just this sum to tell him the secrets of the Casino.

She was about to say an immediate yes when she remembered that warning clause in her contract—a contract that everyone working for the Casino had to sign. No member of the staff should ever talk about the Casino's affairs. The penalty was instant dismissal and possible prosecution.

Seeing her hesitate, Ludovick had said, "I know what you have signed, but you need not be afraid. Think it over. No one will ever know who gave me the information. After all, five hundred dollars is a useful sum. There could be more . . ."

He had got to his feet, smiled at her and walked away, swinging his panama hat, stepping around the large, overfed carcasses of the rich, laid out to broil in the sun with their knotted veins, their hammer toes and their glistening fat.

That evening, when she had had time to think over his suggestion, he had called her on the telephone.

"I have spoken to the Editor. He is quite willing to pay a thousand. I am so pleased. I thought he might be difficult. Now, my pretty, can you help me for one thousand dollars?"

So, with a sick feeling of guilt and of fear of being discovered, she had helped him. He had given her five hundred dollars. The other five hundred would come, he explained with his fatherly smile, when she had given him all the necessary information. And as he probed, his questions becoming more and more disturbing, she had come to realise that he might not be after all a journalist. He might be a man planning to rob the Casino. Why so much interest in the number of guards, the amount of money that went into the vault each night and the security system . . . surely this was the kind of information that a man planning to rob the Casino, would need? Then this final request: the need for the blueprints of the Casino's electrical system. He had asked her for this three afternoons ago while they sat in his shabby Buick coupé on a lonely beach on the outskirts of Paradise City. At this request, she had rebelled.

"Oh, no! I can't give you that! You couldn't possibly want that for an article! I don't understand. I'm beginning to think . . ."

He had smiled a little crookedly, and his dry, clawlike hand had dropped gently on hers, making her draw away and shiver.

"Don't think, my pretty," he said. "I need the blueprints. Don't let us argue about it. My magazine is willing to pay. Shall we say another one thousand dollars?" He drew an envelope from his pocket, "And here is the second five hundred I owe you . . . you see? And now you will have yet another one thousand dollars."

As she took the envelope, crushing it into her bag, she knew this man was really dangerous, that, in spite of his appearance, he was planning a robbery and he was using her to make an impossible robbery possible. If she had another one thousand dollars she wouldn't have to bother to get to the Casino every evening at seven and remain in the vault until three in the morning ever again. She would be free to marry Terry. Her whole drab life would be completely changed.

She abruptly decided if this little man was really planning to rob the Casino, she didn't want to know about it.

But she did want another one thousand dollars. She hesitated for perhaps seventy seconds, then she nodded.

But it wasn't easy. Finally, she did manage to get the blueprint he needed. This was only because she had access to the general office files when she happened to work there during the day for the extra money. This smiling little man had shown his brilliance when he had chosen her to help him. But this man, whose real name was Serge Maisky, was as cunning and as dangerous as a snake. He had come to Paradise City ten months ago. He had watched and inquired discreetly about the four girls who worked in the Casino's vault. He had finally decided to concentrate on this attractive little blonde whose name was Lana Evans. His selection proved that his instinct and judgement were faultless. Lana Evans was to give him the key to the biggest and most spectacular Casino robbery in the history of all Casino robberies.

So now, here they were, face to face, surrounded by a milling crowd of tourists in the dim-lighted Aquarium that housed, among many fish, performing dolphins. He smiled at her, taking her hand in his dry claw and leading her away from the mob to the comparative quietness of a tank that contained a bored, sad-looking octopus.

"Were you successful?"

His smile was as immaculate as his clothes, but Lana Evans could sense his desperate anxiety, and this anxiety made her frightened.

She nodded.

"Splendid." His anxiety turned off like the change from red to green of a traffic light. "I have the money . . . all of it. One thousand beautiful dollars." The grey eyes swept past her, examining the faces of the tourists near them. "Give it to me."

"The money first," Lana Evans said breathlessly. She was very frightened and the dank atmosphere of the cave made her feel faint.

"Of course," He took a fat envelope from his hip pocket. "It is all here. Don't count it now, my pretty. People will see you. Where are the blueprints?"

Her fingers closed over the envelope, feeling the crinkling of the bills, out of sight, but now in her grasp. For a brief moment she wondered if he were cheating her, but decided to take the risk. There seemed a lot of money in the envelope. She wanted to get this dangerous transaction finished quickly. She gave him the blueprint, several pages of complicated electrical wiring that covered all the fuse boxes of the Casino's lighting circuit, the air-conditioning system and the many burglar alarms. He took a very quick look at the pages, half turning, sharing his inspection with the octopus that moved away, taking shelter behind a rock.

"There . . ." He put her betrayal into his hip pocket. "Now we have completed a very happy transaction." He smiled, his slate-grey eyes suddenly remote as buttons of dirty snow. "Oh . . . one more thing . . ."

"No!" Her voice sharpened. "Nothing more! I don't care . . ."

"Please." He raised his hand, placating, soothing. "I'm not asking for anything more. I am very satisfied. You have been so co-operative, so pleasant to work with, so reliable . . . may I make my own personal contribution . . . a modest, trifling gift?" From his pocket, he took a small square packet, neatly tied with red and gold ribbon with a gold label bearing the magic name *Diana*. "Please accept this . . . a pretty girl like you should take care of her hands."

She took the packet, startled by this unexpected kindness. *Diana* hand cream was created and manufactured only for the very rich. Holding the packet in her hand, she felt even richer than he had made her feel when he had given her the envelope.

"Why . . . oh, thanks . . ."

"Thank *you*, my pretty . . . goodbye."

He melted into the crowd like a small, kindly ghost: one moment he was smiling at her, the next he was gone. He disappeared so quickly, it was hard to believe he had ever been standing before her.

A large, red-faced man wearing a yellow and blue flowered shirt appeared before her, grinning.

"I'm Thompson from Minneapolis," he said in a loud,

booming voice. "Have you seen those goddam dolphins? Never seen anything like them in my life!"

She stared blankly at him and edged away, then, when she was sure she was out of reach of his hands, she turned and made her way quietly towards the exit, clutching on to the small box of hand cream in which lay her death.

They came to Paradise City, separately, stealthily, like cautious rats coming out into the sunlight.

At this period of the high season, a constant police watch was kept on the airport and the railroad station. There were also police check points outside the City on the three major highways. Police officers with photographic memories waited at the various barriers, their hard, cop eyes staring searchingly at each passenger coming through the check points. Every now and then a hand would be raised and a passenger stopped. He or she would be whisked out of the slowly moving line of passengers and taken aside.

The dialogue was always the same: "Hello, Jack [or Charlie or Lulu] . . . got a return ticket? Better use it: you're not wanted here."

The same form of dialogue was used at the highway check points and cars were manoeuvred out of the queue and sent back towards Miami.

This police surveillance prevented hundreds of big and small criminals from operating in the City, saving the rich from being fleeced.

So the four men who had come in answer to an intriguing summons and who had been warned of the police cordon came separately and with care.

Jess Chandler, because he had no police record, came by air. This tall, handsome, debonair looking man walked without hesitation towards the police barrier, confident that his false passport and his glibly constructed background of a wealthy coffee grower with estates in Brazil would satisfy the police scrutiny.

At the age of thirty-nine, Chandler was now recognised by the underworld as one of the slickest and smartest con men in the racket. He traded on his movie-star appearance. His lean brown face, his short nose and full lips, his high cheekbones and his large, dark eyes gave him a sensual, swashbuckling look of a confident womaniser, and some of the women, looking at him, knew this, feeling a pang of desire as they moved with him in the long queue towards the heat and the sunshine that waited for them outside the airport building.

The two waiting police officers regarded him. Chandler stared back at them, his eyes bored, his expression slightly contemptuous. He showed no fear and fear was what the officers were looking for. After only a brief glance at his passport, they waved him through to the waiting line of taxis.

Chandler hefted his handbag from one hand to the other and grinned. He knew it would be easy . . . it had been easy.

Mish Collins had to be much more careful. He had only been out of jail for two months and every cop house had his photograph. It had taken him some hours to make up his mind how best he could get past the police cordon without being asked awkward questions. Finally, he had joined a sight-seeing tour that left Miami for a tour of the Everglades and then finally a night at Paradise City, before returning to Miami. In the packed coach, loaded with noisy, happy, slightly drunk tourists, he felt comparatively safe. He had brought his harmonica with him. Ten minutes before reaching the police check point, he had begun to play to the delight of his companions. The instrument, cupped in his huge, fleshy hands, completely shielded his face. He had picked a seat with three other big fleshy men at the back of the coach and the police officer who climbed into the coach merely glanced at him, then concentrated on the other sweating, bovine faces that all grinned back at him.

In this way, Mish Collins arrived safely in Paradise City, a man who the police would have immediately turned back had he been recognised, for Mish Collins was not only one of the top safe blowers in the country, but had also earned a reputation that made many burglar alarm manufacturers quail with apprehension.

Mish Collins was forty-one years of age. He had spent fifteen years of his life in and out of jail. He was massively built, fat, with a lumpy muscular body of great strength. His red hair was beginning to thin and there were lines of hard living, deeply etched on his coarse, rubbery face. His small, restless eyes had a cocky, cheerful light of cunning that somehow made the unwary take to him.

When the bus pulled into the bus station, he drew the Courier aside and told him he wouldn't be taking the return journey.

"I've remembered I have a buddy here," he explained. "You cash in my return ticket and keep the change for yourself. You certainly have earned it," and before the Courier could even thank him, Mish had disappeared into the swirling crowd.

Jack Perry came in his own Oldsmobile Cutlass convertible, now a little shabby, but still a nice looking car. He was aware that the finger-print department at Washington had one of his finger-prints; only one, the right forefinger, and this was the only mistake he had ever made during a long life of crime, a secret he kept to himself like a man nursing a cancer. At least, they had no photograph of him so he approached the police check point satisfied that the two bulls checking the cars would have no idea they were about to encounter a professional killer.

For the past twenty-seven years, Perry had earned a living by hiring out his gun. He was an expert shot, utterly amoral, and human life to him meant as little as something he might have stepped in on the sidewalk. But he was a free spender and was always short of money: women played a major rôle in his life . . . and when there were women, you spent money.

He was around sixty-two years of age: a short, heavily built man with close-cut, snow-white hair, a round fattish face, wide-spaced eyes under bushy white eyebrows, a thin mouth and a small hooked nose. He dressed conservatively. Now, he was wearing a slate-grey tropical suit, a blood-red tie and a cream-coloured panama hat. He was always smiling, a grimace more than a smile, and if he had had any friends he would have been nicknamed 'Smiler', but he had no friends. He was a solitary, ruthless killer without a soul, and with no feeling for anyone, not even himself.

He drew up behind the car in front of him and waited while the two police officers checked the papers of the passengers. Then, when they waved the car on, Perry let the Cutlass creep up to the waiting men.

He regarded them with his fixed grin.

"Hi, fellas," he said, waving a fat hand. "Have I done something wrong?"

Patrol Officer Fred O'Toole had been on duty now for the past four hours. He was a big, dark Irishman with alert, bleak eyes. He was sick to death of all the people who had crawled past his check point in their luxury cars with their corny jokes, their servile smiles, their contempt and often their arrogance. They were all heading for a good time: gambling, the best food, the best hotels, the best whores while he stood with burning feet in the hot evening sun waving them through, knowing as soon as they were out of his hearing, they would make some derogatory remark about this goddam Mick sonofabitch.

O'Toole took an immediate dislike to this fat, elderly, grinning man. He had no real reason for this dislike, but the grin, the empty washed-out blue eyes made his hackles rise.

"Got a passport?" he snapped, resting his gloved hand on the car's window frame and glaring down at Perry.

"What do I want a passport for?" Perry said. "I've got a licence . . . that do?"

O'Toole held out his hand.

Perry gave him the licence that had cost him four hundred dollars: an expensive little item, but worth it. The right forefinger print had been most skilfully altered, and such alterations cost money.

"What's your business here?"

"Plenty of eating, plenty of gambling and plenty of girls," Perry said and laughed. "I'm on vacation, buddy . . . and boy! am I going to have me a vacation!"

O'Toole continued to glare at him, but he handed back the licence. Jackson, the other patrol officer, looking at the big hold-up O'Toole was causing by his questions, said testily, "Aw, for Pete's sake, Fred, there's a mile of the bastards still waiting."

O'Toole stepped back and waved Perry on. Perry's grin widened, his foot squeezed down on the gas pedal, and the Cutlass gathered speed.

Well, he had made it, he thought, as he snapped on the radio. He had fooled those two jerks and now . . . Paradise City, here I come!

Washington Smith had to be much more careful how he arrived in the City. Negroes weren't encouraged anyway even if they were respectable, and Washington Smith was now far from being respectable. He had been out of jail for two weeks. His crime was hitting two police officers who had cornered him and were about to put the boot in. He had been stupid enough to have taken part in a freedom-to-vote march. The march had been ruthlessly broken up, the marchers scattered and because Wash—as his friends called him—was a little guy, two big cops had chased him up a cul-de-sac and had got set to have themselves a ball. But Wash happened to be a welter-weight contender for the Golden Gloves. Instead of meekly accepting the beating, he flattened both officers with two beautiful left hooks to their jaws. Then he had run, but not far. A bullet in his leg brought him down, and a club descending on his head knocked him unconscious. He drew eight months for resisting arrest and he had come out of jail savage and determined that from now on he would be an enemy of the Whites.

When he received the summons to Paradise City, he had hesitated. Could this be a trap? he had asked himself. The message was brief.

> *A very profitable job is waiting to be done. Mish recommends you. Be at The Black Crab Restaurant at 22.00 hrs on 20th February if you are* INTERESTED IN MAKING A VERY LARGE SUM OF MONEY. *The inclosed is for your travelling expenses. Police watch all entrances to the City. Be careful. Ask for Mr. Ludovick.*

It could be a hoax, Wash had thought, but an expensive one. There had been two one-hundred dollar bills inside the envelope. Besides, he knew Mish Collins whom he had met in jail and whom he liked and respected. A very large sum of money! That's what he needed right now. Without big money, a negro had no life of his own. He decided he had nothing to lose.

He arrived in Paradise City under a load of crates of lettuces on their way to the Paradise-Ritz Hotel. He had lain hidden as the truck had been waved through the police check point, his heart thumping, his nerves crawling.

So he, like the other three, beat the police cordon set up to protect the rich of Paradise City.

The first move in Serge Maisky's plan to rob the richest Casino in the world had succeeded.

The Black Crab Restaurant was contained in a three-storey wooden building, built on stilts, thirty yards into the sea and reached by a narrow jetty. It was the meeting place for the sponge divers of the Florida Marine Manufacturing Co., and very few tourists, and certainly none of the residents of Seacombe, ever visited the place. It was notorious for heavy drinking, brawls and excellent sea food.

On the top floor of the building there were three private dining-rooms. They were reached by an outside staircase, and people with important matters to discuss could be sure of complete privacy. The negro waiter who officiated on the third floor was a deaf-mute.

In the largest of the private dining-rooms that had a view of the distant lights of Paradise City and the harbour with its anchored yachts, preparations had been completed for a dinner of five covers.

Mish Collins was the first to arrive. Jos, the negro waiter, regarded him, nodded, and then silently handed him a tumbler containing a treble rum, lime and cracked ice.

Perry and Chandler arrived together, and, a minute or so later, Washington Smith slid uneasily into the room.

Mish took over the duties of the host.

"Welcome, fellas," he said. "Make yourselves at home. The dinge is deaf and dumb. Don't worry about him." He beamed at Wash, holding out his hand. "H'yah, bud. Long time no see."

Wash shook hands, nodding, while Perry eyed him with a quizzing, bleak stare.

Chandler refused the rum and lime, and asked for a whisky and soda. Jos stared blankly at him, then returned to his task of opening oysters that lay in a tub of ice.

"Help yourself," Mish said. "The stuff's all there. I told you, didn't I . . . he's a deaf-mute."

Still staring at Wash, Perry said, "Who's he? What's he doing here?"

"What are we all doing here?" Mish said and laughed. "Sit down, fellas. Let's get to know each other." He pointed to Chandler who had made his drink and was now looking out of the window at the view. "He's Jess." The thick finger pointed to Washington Smith. "He's Wash." He nodded to Perry. "That's Jack. I guess you all know who I am. Come on, fellas, relax," and he went over to a chair and sat down.

Wash had refused a drink. He stood uneasily by the door. He was always awkward and on the defensive in the company of Whites.

Perry chose a chair away from Mish. He sat down, nursing his drink, a dead cigar gripped firmly between his small white teeth.

"What's this—a party?" he asked, his washed-out blue eyes flickering around the room.

"That's it," Mish said happily. "A party."

Chandler turned. His handsome face showed irritation. "Do you know anything about this deal?"

"Not much."

"Who is this guy Ludovick?"

"Yeah . . . I know about him." Mish shook his head in awe. "Sure, I can tell you about him. For one thing, that's not his name. His name is Serge Maisky. I met him in Roxburgh jail. He had a job there . . . dispenser."

"What the hell's that . . . a dispenser?" Perry demanded.

"He was in charge of the pill and drug joint in the prison," Mish explained. "The croaker ordered you a pill and Maisky supplied it. He worked there for ten years . . . a real, bright boy. He and I got pretty pally. I'm a great one for pills. Before he retired, he told me he had an idea for the biggest take of all takes. He told me when he had set it up he would send for me and he wanted three others. I picked you three. You can thank me later." Mish's rubbery face creased into a broad grin. "I'll tell you this, fellas. This little guy looks harmless, but, boy, he's as harmless as a rattlesnake, and brains . . . ! He's the original H. bomb! I'll tell you this: when he says the take is big, I'm sold. That's why I'm here. I don't know what the job is, but . . ."

"That's why *I* am here . . . to tell you," Maisky said gently from the door.

Perry stiffened. His hand moved for a brief moment towards his hidden gun. Chandler gave a start that slopped his drink. Wash stepped quickly away from the door. Mish was the only calm one: he continued to grin.

Maisky shut the door. He shook his head at Jos as the negro reached for a glass, then he regarded the four men steadily, slowly in turn.

"Gentlemen," he said in his quiet, clear voice, "I am

very happy to meet you. I hope none of you had any trouble getting here." The grey eyes probed. "Did you?"

The four men shook their heads.

"Excellent. Then let us eat. I am sure you must be hungry. Then, and not until then, we will discuss business."

An hour later, Mish pushed back his chair and released a soft belch.

"Fine meal," he said. "Pretty different to the slop we got at Roxie, huh, doc?"

Maisky smiled.

"Let us forget those painful memories." He lit a cigarette, offered his pack to Wash who shook his head, then seeing Perry was lighting a cigar and Mish and Chandler were already smoking, he returned the pack to his pocket.

During the meal, Maisky had dominated the four men. His quiet, gentle manner baffled them, except Mish who knew him and beamed on him like a proud mother displaying her brilliant child. Maisky talked of politics, travel and women. Words flowed from him, but every now and then, he would ask an abrupt, probing question of one of the men, listen carefully to the answer, then continue his monologue. He ate very little, but during the hour, he succeeded in some miraculous manner to reduce tension, to get the four men at ease with one another. Even Wash was now relaxed.

When the deaf-mute had cleared the table and set two bottles of whisky, ice and glasses within reach and had gone, Maisky cupped his pointed chin in his clawlike hands and said, "Well now, gentlemen, let us talk business. I have a proposition to make to you. Mish may have told you that for three years he and I were in contact. I have yet to meet a man who can swallow so many pills as Mish. During the time we were together, I formed the opinion that he is a very clever technician, and I learned he knew other technicians. This is why I asked him to contact you gentlemen. As for Wash . . . he is not quite like us. He isn't a criminal." The gentle smile broadened, "but he is necessary to my plan and he needs money and he has a grudge."

The other men looked at Wash who eyed them uneasily. Chandler crushed out his cigarette impatiently.

"Who cares?" he said. "Let's hear the proposition. What's all this crap about the biggest take?"

Maisky's expression was benign, but reproving.

"Please . . . I know you have had many successes, my friend, but try to be patient with me. This is a team . . . we must understand each other, and we must work closely together or we will fail."

"What's the proposition?" Chandler repeated.

"We are here to take two million dollars from the Casino," Maisky said.

There was a long pause of absolute silence. Even Mish suddenly lost his smile of confidence. The four men stared at Maisky with startled, unbelieving eyes.

"Two million dollars?" Chandler said, the first to recover. "Look, I have things to do. What the hell is this pipe dream . . . two million dollars?"

Maisky waved his hand to the whisky.

"Please, help yourselves, gentlemen. Unhappily, I can't . . . doctor's orders." He turned to Perry. "You heard what I said. Jess, I can see, doesn't believe me . . . do you?"

Perry blew a thin cloud of cigar smoke towards the ceiling.

"Keep talking," he said. "Don't worry about buddy boy. He's a natural worrier. You keep talking. I'm listening."

Chandler swung around and stared at Perry who stared back. His washed-out blue eyes sent a prickle of fear up Chandler's spine. He wasn't a man of violence and the look Perry gave him chilled him. With a forced, indifferent shrug, he reached for the whisky bottle.

"Okay . . . then talk," he said.

Maisky settled back in his chair.

"For years I have dreamed of finding the big take," he said. "With a few well-chosen men, who know their job, I have finally decided the big take is right here. We can take two million dollars out of the Casino, but only if you all have the necesssary nerve, and if you will do exactly what I tell you. If you can't conform to these two simple rules, then let us forget it." His eyes, now ice cold, stared fixedly at each man in turn before he said, "Can you conform?"

Mish said, "Anything you say, doc, I go for. You count me in."

Maisky ignored him, he was staring at Chandler.

"You?"

"Rob the Casino?" Chandler said. "It can't be done. A couple of years ago, a guy put up the very same proposition to me. He thought of walking in there with ten men, but we . . ."

Maisky's smile of contempt stopped him. Again the two men looked at each other, then Chandler said, "Well, okay, if you think you're that smart, I'll listen, but I tell you they have twenty picked guards, foolproof alarm systems and the cops are watching the place all the time . . . but okay, I'll listen."

Maisky said gently, "You must do more than that, Jess. You are either in or you're out . . . now."

Chandler hesitated, then waved his hand in assent. He suddenly realised he was dealing with someone as deadly as Perry, and he knew all about Perry.

"Okay . . . okay . . . count me in. I still think it isn't possible, but if you think it is, then I'll go along with you."

Maisky looked at Perry who grinned at him.

"Sure, I'm with you. Just tell me," he said.

Maisky looked at Wash.

"And you?"

The little negro shifted in his chair, but only because the other men were staring at him and he was always uncomfortable when white men stared at him. He didn't hesitate when he said, "Of course . . . what have I to lose?"

Maisky sat back, smiling.

"That is very satisfactory. Then I take it, if you are convinced, gentlemen, I can rely on you?" He waited long enough for the four men to nod, then he went on, "Well now, have a drink while I tell you how it can be done."

There was a brief pause as the men re-filled their glasses. Mish offered Wash the bottle of whisky, but he shook his head. They lit cigarettes, sat back and waited, regarding Maisky as he took a thick folder of papers from his hip pocket.

"First, let me tell you a little about the Casino," he said, laying the papers on the table before him. "This is the high season. On Saturday—the day after tomorrow—there will be something like three million dollars in cash in the building. If we get all the breaks, we should get away with two million. Two million dollars split up amongst the five of us makes three hundred thousand dollars each man."

Chandler said sharply, "Not by my arithmetic. I make it four hundred thousand!"

Maisky smiled gently.

"You are quite right, but I will have the major share. You will each have three hundred thousand and I will have the rest because I have had a lot of expenses. I have thought of the plan, I have arranged how it is to be carried out and, if it interests you, I have spent the past nine months in the City. I have had to hire this bungalow and I have had to pay out a considerable sum for information. So . . ." He waved his clawlike hands. "I have the major share."

"Sure, doc," Mish said. "That's fair enough. Three hundred thousand dollars! Gee! That's the kind of money I've always dreamed about!"

"You haven't got it yet," Chandler said.

Maisky leaned forward.

"May I continue? Let me explain about the Casino. Jess says he has already considered robbing the place with ten men walking into the gambling rooms." He laughed. "Well, of course that would not have produced results. On Saturday night, the maximum amount of money on the tables will be around a quarter of a million. The rest of the money remains in the vault immediately below the gambling rooms. When more money is needed, it is sent up in small box elevators. Two armed guards remain by each elevator during the gambling session. When money accumulates on the tables, it is sent down to the vaults. So there is a constant coming and going of money . . . up and down . . . and always heavily guarded." He paused to light another cigarette, then went on, "It became obvious to me after a few days' watching this routine that the vault itself must be our attacking point. Here, the money is kept very neatly. There are four girls in the vault and two armed guards. The girls handle the money: the guards keep watch. The vault is protected by a steel door and no one is allowed to enter except on official business. This has been going on for years. Here is the soft underbelly. So we will get into the vault, take the money and walk out."

He made another deliberate pause while he looked at the four men. Mish scowled and began to scratch his head. Wash sat motionless, his black face expressionless. Perry continued to stare up at the ceiling. Plans like this bored him. All he wanted was to be told what to do and then to go into action. Chandler stared at Maisky as if he thought he was crazy.

"Oh, for Pete's sake!" he said. "Is this a theory? You haven't a hope in hell of getting into that vault. What are you doing . . . having a game with us?"

Maisky took from his jacket pocket a shiny, steel cylinder no more than six inches long. He placed it on the table with the finicky care of a man displaying an artistic masterpiece.

"This is the answer to the problem," he said. "With this, we will have no trouble removing the money from the vault."

The four men stared at the shiny cylinder on the table.

After a pause, Perry said, "Just what the hell is that?"

"It contains a paralysing gas," Maisky said. "It is quite ingenious and it's under tremendous pressure. It is effective within ten seconds."

Chandler rubbed the back of his neck as he eyed Maisky. "Is it . . . lethal?"

"Oh no. After four or five hours its effects wear off.

We are robbing the Casino, my friend, not committing mayhem."

"Well, what do you know? That's mighty cute," Perry said. "Go on . . . tell us more."

Maisky picked up the papers on the table and handed them to Mish.

"Look at these. Do they mean anything to you?"

Mish leaned back in his chair and studied the blueprints of the Casino's electrical circuits. It took him only a few seconds to realise what he was looking at and he glanced up, his red face alight with a grin of admiration.

"I take my hat off to you, doc. Sure, I get it now. How did you get hold of this little lot?"

Maisky shrugged.

"As I told you, I have been here for nine months and I have not wasted my time."

Chandler peered over Mish's shoulder, then he looked at Maisky.

"You've certainly been working at this thing, but I'm not sold yet. Just what do we have to do?" he said.

"Here is the general plan. The Casino shuts at three a.m. At two-thirty a.m. most of the money will have been returned to the vault. This is the time for our attack. Here is what happens in outline. At two-thirty precisely, Mish will walk into the Casino wearing the uniform of the City's Electricians. This uniform I have already obtained. He will say there is an electrical fault and he wants to check the fuse boxes. At this hour, there will only be a stooge in control. I have been to the Casino every night since I have been here and I know at one forty-five the general office shuts down. Harry Lewis, who is in charge of the Casino, is always moving around in the gambling rooms at this time until the Casino shuts. His secretaries have gone home. So you will have no trouble. The stooge in the lobby will assume Lewis has called you and he will show you where to find the fuse boxes. You will have to be careful about the timing, Mish. Now look at the blueprint. First, I want the air conditioner in the vault cut off."

The other men watched as Mish studied the blueprint. After a few moments, he looked up and nodded.

"Can do . . . it's easy."

"Yes . . . I thought it might be with you handling it." Maisky's voice was gentle and confident. "Then there is a calculator in the vault which the girls use to add up the total take. This also must be put on the blink. I believe you will see the fuse box for that."

Mish nodded after examining the blueprint.

"Sure," he said. "No trouble."

"So this is your job, Mish. You put the air conditioner and the calculator on the blink. I'm just giving you this in outline. Later, of course, we will go into details. Now . . ." he looked at Chandler. "You have a more difficult rôle to play. You and Wash will arrive exactly at two-thirty in a small truck . . . I have the truck in my garage. You both will be wearing the uniforms of I.B.M. engineers, and you will have with you a carton that is supposed to contain a calculator. It will not, of course, contain a calculator. It will contain two gas masks and two automatic pistols. These articles I have already obtained. Jess will tell the doorman who guards the entrance to the vault that he has had a call from Mr. Lewis to replace the calculator in the vault. While he is talking to the doorman, Mish will put the calculator in the vault on the blink. So when Jess and Wash arrive at the door to the vault, the guards will know the calculator has broken down. It is up to Jess to talk his way into the vault . . . it shouldn't be too difficult. Both he and Wash will be wearing the appropriate uniforms and carrying a carton marked on all sides: I.B.M. The girls will be complaining that their machine is out of order. Psychologically, I think we can get away with this. Once inside, Chandler will open the carton and hold up the guards. Wash will put on his gas mask and then take over from Chandler who will also put on his gas mask. This must be done very quickly and with a lot of menace. We will, of course, practice this tomorrow. Before the guards have time to start trouble, Jess will release the gas.

This is very simple to do. A sharp tap on any solid object . . . the table . . . the wall . . . anything solid, will set it off. In ten seconds there will be no opposition. The vault will be filled with the gas. You two will then fill the carton with as much money as you can lay hands on . . . and there will be plenty. You will choose only five-hundred-dollar bills. These bills will be in packets and will be easy to handle. Having filled the carton, you will walk out. The doorman will assume you are taking away the calculator that has broken down. You will put the carton into the truck and then we will all drive off. This is a very brief summary of my plan. The details, of course, will have to be fully discussed and rehearsed, but we will do this tomorrow night." He sat back, tapped ash off his cigarette and looked inquiringly at the four men who had been listening with absorbed concentration.

Perry said, "Just where do I come in on the set-up?"

"Ah, yes . . . you." Maisky smiled at him. "You will also be wearing the I.B.M. uniform. You will come in with Jess and Wash, but you will stay with the doorman. I'll tell you about him later. He is an old man who likes to talk. Your job is to talk to him. I don't anticipate trouble, but we must be ready to deal with it should it occur. Some nosy guard might turn up and start being awkward." Maisky stared fixedly at Perry. "I am relying on you to take care of trouble and of nosy guards."

Perry grinned.

"Fine . . . if that's all I have to do, it's easy."

Chandler said sharply, "We now know what Mish, Wash, Jack and I have to do. Just exactly what will you do?"

"I will drive the truck," Maisky said. "I am a lot older than any of you and I don't propose to take too active a part in this operation. We will have to make a quick getaway, so I feel I am quite capable of handling the truck." He paused, waited, then went on when none of the men said anything. "There is one thing we must accept. The news of the robbery will break very quickly. The Chief of Police here is very efficient. We would be asking for trouble if we tried to leave the City with the money until the heat dies down. The money will be buried in my garden. We will then split up, take a vacation in the City, then, when the heat is off, we will take our shares and leave in our own separate ways."

Perry said, "I don't like that. We will split the money at once and each of us will be responsible for taking care of his own share."

Chandler said, "Yes."

After hesitating, Mish said, "Well, I guess that's right."

Maisky shrugged.

"As you like, gentlemen. We will, of course, work out all the details later. But I take it, you approve of the general plan?"

"It's great," Mish said.

Maisky looked at Wash.

"And you?"

"Oh, yes . . . I will do exactly what you tell me," Wash said. "I think it is good."

Chandler said, "There's one thing that fazes me . . . just how did you get this blueprint and all your information? Whom did you buy it from?"

Maisky regarded the glowing end of his cigarette.

"I wonder if you really want to know, my friend?" he said. "You need have no fear about my informant. I have taken care of that very minor problem." He looked up suddenly and Chandler flinched away as he looked into the grey, ice-cold eyes.

two

HARRY LEWIS, Director of the Casino, neatly parked his black Fleetwood Cadillac in a vacant parking bay outside police headquarters, cut the engine and slid out into the early morning sunshine.

Lewis, tall, thin, elegantly dressed, was moving into his late fifties. He had been in charge of the richest Casino in the world now for fifteen years. He had the air of affluence and supreme confidence that only a background of extreme wealth can give a man.

He walked up the steps and into the Charge Room, where the desk sergeant, Charlie Tanner, was coping with a mass of drunk-in-charge-of-a-car reports.

Seeing Lewis, Tanner dropped the reports and jumped to his feet.

"'Morning, Mr. Lewis. Something I can do?"

Lewis always received V.I.P. treatment from the police. They were well aware of his generosity at Christmas and Thanksgiving Day. Every detective and every patrolman received a sixteen-pound turkey and a bottle of Scotch on these two festivals, and they realised this generosity must cost a whale of a lot of money.

"The Chief in?" Lewis asked.

"Sure, Mr. Lewis. You go right on up," Tanner said.

"How's your wife, Charlie?"

Tanner grinned happily. This was another thing about Lewis. He seemed to know everything about everyone in Paradise City. Tanner's wife had just come out of hospital after a difficult miscarriage.

"Fine now, Mr. Lewis . . . and thanks."

"You must take care of her, Charles," Lewis said. "We men take our wives too much for granted. Where would we be without them?" He flicked a folded bill across the desk. "Fuss her . . . women like being fussed."

He walked over to the stairway that led to Chief of Police Terrell's office. Tanner's eyes grew round when he saw the bill was for $20.

Lewis tapped on Terrell's door, pushed it open and walked into the small, sparsely furnished room.

Chief of Police Terrell, a massively built man with sandy hair, turning white at the temples and a jutting, aggressive jaw was pouring coffee from a carton into two paper cups. Sergeant Joe Beigler, his right-hand man, watched the coffee with an eye of an addict while he rested his big frame in a creaking, upright chair. Both men stiffened as Lewis walked casually into the little room. Beigler got to his feet. Terrell reached for another paper cup, smiling.

"Hello, Harry . . . you're early," he said. "Have some coffee?"

Lewis took Beigler's chair, shaking his head.

"You two . . . you seem to live on coffee," he said. "Busy?"

Terrell lifted his massive shoulders.

"We're starting the day . . . nothing very special. Something on your mind?"

Lewis selected a cigarette from a gold case. Beigler was quick to give him a light.

"At this time of the season, Frank, I have always plenty

on my mind," he said. "But tomorrow's something special. I thought it would be an idea to talk to you. Tomorrow, we are expecting twenty top-class gamblers from the Argentine who are really out to win some money from us. These boys don't give a damn how much they lose. We have the job of covering their play. There will be a lot of money in the Casino and I thought some police protection might be sound. Think you can help me?"

Terrell sipped his coffee, then nodded.

"Of course. What do you want, Harry?"

"I am moving three million dollars in cash from the bank to the Casino tomorrow morning. I'll have four of my guards with the truck, but I would also like a police escort. That's a lot of money, and I want to be sure it arrives all in one piece."

"That's easy. We'll have six men with you," Terrell said.

"Thanks, Frank, I knew I could rely on you. Then I would like three or four of your men at the Casino in the evening. I don't anticipate trouble. I have twenty good men of my own, but I think it would have a depressing effect on anyone with ambitions to see the police were around too."

"I'll fix that. You can have Lepski and four patrolmen."

Lewis nodded.

"Lepski would be just the man. Well, thanks, Frank." He tapped ash off his cigarette, then went on, "What's the situation like? Anyone here I should know about?"

"No. We have had a number of hopefuls, but they have been recognised and turned back. From the reports I've been looking at, we haven't one really dangerous specimen in town." Terrell finished his coffee and began to fill his pipe. "You can relax, Harry. I'm satisfied. We have really been working on this thing. There is, of course, the odd chance that some amateur might have a try at you, but with the extra precautions, you don't need to worry." He regarded Lewis thoughtfully. "You have no reason to worry, have you?"

"No reason . . . I worry just the same."

"Well, don't. What time are you collecting the money from the bank?"

"Ten-thirty sharp."

"Okay. I'll have my men at the bank and they will escort you. Okay?"

Lewis got to his feet.

"I think I will relax," he said and shook hands.

When he had gone, Beigler reached for the carton of coffee.

"Three million dollars!" His voice was outraged. "What a goddam waste of money! Think what one could do with that dough . . . and it's going to be used to give a bunch of Spicks a thrill."

Terrell eyed him, then nodded.

"It's their money, Joe. It's our job to take care of it for them." He flicked down the switch on his inter-com. "Charles? Where's Lepski? I want him."

At seven o'clock on this Friday morning, Serge Maisky got out of bed, put on the coffee percolator and then took a shower. He shaved with a cut-throat razor, dressed, then went into the small kitchen and poured himself a cup of coffee. Carrying the cup into the shabby living-room, he sat down and sipped the coffee.

So far, he decided, everything was going according to plan. Jess Chandler was staying at the Beach Hotel. Perry was at the Bay Hotel, Mish Collins was at the Sunshine Hotel and Wash was at the Welcome Motel. Tonight, the four men would come to his bungalow and rehearse their particular jobs. He was now satisfied, having met the men, that he had a team he could rely on. Mish Collins' choice had been sound.

He finished his coffee, washed up the cup and saucer, then went to a closet where he had stored two five-gallon plastic containers. These he filled with water from the kitchen tap. He then collected a fair-sized carton full of canned food from another closet in the kitchen. He carried the carton to his Buick and put it in the boot. He then went back and carried out the two plastic containers which he also put in the boot.

His movements were slow and deliberate. He was feeling his years. He was sharply conscious that he was sixty-two and exertion of any kind didn't agree with him.

He paused for a long moment to make certain he had forgotten nothing, then, remembering the batteries for his flashlight, he collected them from the drawer in his living-room and now decided he was ready to go.

He locked the door of his bungalow and then walked to his car, slid under the driving wheel and started the motor.

Thirty minutes later on the highway out of Seacombe, which was a suburb of Paradise City, Maisky edged the car on to the far right-hand lane, then swung off on to a dirt road that led in a climbing drive into the pine forest that circled the outskirts of Seacombe and Paradise City.

The road was narrow and he drove with care. One never knew, even at this early hour, if someone might come belting down the road which was scarcely wide enough to take two cars. But he met no one. Finally, after driving through the forest for twenty minutes, he again swung off the dirt road and on to a narrow track, leading into the depths of the forest. He slowed long enough to inspect the sign that he himself had painted and erected two days ago. The sign read: *Game Preserve. Private. Keep out.* He gave a nod of approval as he continued up the track. The sign was weathering. He had to admit it was well executed, and it looked convincing.

A few seconds later, he slowed the car and then edged it off the track, bumping over the hard, dry ground into a small glade which he had discovered during his thorough search of the district for a safe hide. Here, he had already built a canopy of tree branches and uprooted shrubs: a task that had taken him several days. Under this canopy, he drove the Buick. Getting out, he took from the boot the water containers, paused long enough to assure himself that he was completely on his own, then, walking at a steady pace, he moved out of the glade, brushing through the undergrowth, and climbed a path that led to a tree-covered hill.

A two-minutes slow walk, leaving him slightly breathless, brought him to a mass of dead wood, branches and brown leaves. He pulled some of the branches aside, then, ducking under them, he moved into a dark, dank-smelling cave, completely hidden by the camouflage of branches he had erected during the past week.

He paused in the cave to get his breath back. He was a little disturbed that he was so breathless, and there was a small, but ominous pain nagging in his chest. He set down the water containers, then waited. A few minutes later, he began to breathe more freely, and he took out his flashlight and turned the powerful beam around the cave.

Well, he thought, I can't expect miracles. I am getting old. I am doing too much, but at least, so far, everything is going the way I have planned it.

He swung the beam of the flashlight on the sleeping bag, the stores of provisions, the transistor radio and the medical chest: the necessities he had put in this small cave for a six-week stay.

He went to the entrance of the cave to listen, then, satisfied that he was entirely on his own, he went down to the car to collect the rest of the things he had brought with him. Once again, he made his journey up to the cave, moving more slowly, feeling the growing heat of the sun now on his back as he climbed the hill.

Again he checked the contents of the cave to satisfy himself that he had forgotten nothing. Then nodding, he went outside, and very carefully arranged the tree branches to hide completely the entrance.

He went down to the Buick, got in, looked up at the mass of branches and dead leaves that shielded his hideout, nodded his approval, then, reversing the car, he drove back to his bungalow at Seacombe.

* * *

Lana Evans opened her eyes, blinked at the sunlight coming through the yellow blind, moaned a little, and then turned over, hugging the pillow to her. But in a few moments she was wide awake. She sat up in bed and looked at the bedside clock. The time was ten minutes after nine o'clock.

She flicked back the sheet, swung her legs to the floor and went into the bathroom. Her toilet completed, she came back into the dreary little sleeping-cum-living-room and went to the chest of drawers. From under her meagre stock of linen, she took out a roll of $100 bills. She got back to bed and surveyed her fortune. She felt the blood move through her with excitement, but it was an excitement mixed with fear. Suppose someone at the Casino found out what she had told this little man? She was now certain he was planning to rob the Casino. She looked at the money and forced herself to shrug her shoulders. After all, the Casino could afford to lose money. They were stinking rich and she . . . Then she moved uneasily, frowning. How to explain to Terry how she had suddenly acquired all this money? That wasn't going to be easy. Terry was jealous. He suspected every man working at the Casino was after her . . . in a way, he was right, they were, but she wasn't after them. This, he found difficult to believe. She would have to be very careful how she explained to him about her sudden wealth. The money, exciting at first, now began to worry her. She got out of bed and re-hid the money under the freshly laundered bed linen.

She went over to the window and drew up the blind. She looked down at the distant sea, the sun reflecting on the still, blue water and the sailing boats with their yellow and red sails moving out of the harbour.

If only she could tell Terry the truth, she thought, but he was so dreadfully correct. No, this was something she had to keep to herself. She got back into bed and her eyes alighted on the box of *Diana* hand cream. She picked it up and undid the wrapping.

He may be a crook, she thought, but he has style.

She no longer believed in the *New Yorker* myth. He had given her two thousand dollars—an enormous sum to her—for information which she had given him. This was a transaction that would ride rough shod over her conscience for the rest of her life. But this little box of hand cream—the de luxe of de luxe hand creams—must mean that there was a lot of kindness in him, even if he had lied, bribed and corrupted her.

She unscrewed the cap and regarded the white cream ointment that smelt faintly of crushed orchids. With infinite care and with pleasure she spread the deadly cream over her hands. But she found herself a little depressed that this luxury treatment didn't give her the pleasure she hoped it would. Her mind was too occupied. She put the cap back on the jar and the jar back on the bedside table. She began again to concentrate on the problem of how to convince Terry that there was no man involved in her sudden wealth.

Later, still worrying, she shut her eyes and dozed. She kept telling herself that it would work out all right and she would convince Terry. Sometime this afternoon, she would go to an Estate Agent and inquire about a one-room apartment.

An hour later, not aware that she had fallen asleep, she woke with a sudden start, feeling surprisingly cold. Puzzled, she looked at the bedside clock to see it was now twenty minutes to eleven. She thought of a cup of coffee, but she now had no inclination to get out of bed. She not only felt chilly, but lazy and torpid. This growing feeling of chill alerted her . . . was she becoming ill?

Then suddenly, without warning, bile rushed into her mouth and, before she could control the spasm, she vomited over the bedclothes. She felt her hands had turned to fire.

Alarmed, she tried to throw off the bedclothes and get out of bed, but the effort was too much for her.

Her body was now icy cold and clammy and yet her hands burned, and there was a terrible burning sensation in her throat.

What is happening to me? she thought, terrified. Her heart was racing and she had difficulty in breathing.

She forced herself out of bed, but her legs wouldn't support her. She folded up on the floor, her hand vainly reaching towards the telephone that stood on a near-by table.

She opened her mouth to scream for help, but a disgusting, evil-smelling bile choked her, rising into her mouth, down her nostrils and on to her pink, shortie night-dress.

The black, sleek Persian cat who she fed as a routine of love every morning came to the open window thirty minutes later. The cat paused expectantly, regarded the still body lying in a patch of sunlight, twitched its whiskers, then dropped from the window into the room with a solid plop of paws.

With the selfish indifference that is natural to a cat, it walked purposefully to the refrigerator in the kitchen. It sat before the refrigerator, waiting with anxious impatience.

At eight-thirty p.m. Harry Lewis left his office, took the red velvet-lined elevator down to the second floor, nodding to the boy who ran the elevator.

The boy, immaculate in the bottle-green and cream uniform of the Casino, his hands in white cotton gloves, his tanned face shiny, ducked his head, gratified to be recognised.

This was Lewis's favourite hour when the Casino began to come alive. He liked nothing better than to go out on to the big, overhanging balcony and look down on the terrace below, where his clients were drinking, talking and relaxing before going to the restaurant and then into the gambling rooms.

The full moon made the sea a glittering, still lake of silver. It was a warm night with a slight breeze that moved the palm trees, surrounding the terrace.

He stood for a long moment, his hands resting on the

balustrade, as he looked down at the crowded tables below. He saw Fred, the head barman, moving from table to table, taking orders, passing them to his various waiters, pausing to make a discreet joke or to exchange a word with an habitué, but always efficient, seeing that no guest had to wait for a drink.

"Mr. Lewis . . ."

Lewis turned, raising his eyebrows. This was his ritual moment when he disliked being disturbed, but seeing the pretty, dark girl at his side, he smiled. Rita Wallace was in charge of the vault. She had worked now for Lewis for five years, and he had found her completely dependable, supervising the work of the vault with a calm, efficient manner that make the exacting work easy for the other girls.

"Why, Rita . . . good evening." Lewis regarded her. "Something wrong?" He asked the question automatically. He never saw Rita unless there was some problem she couldn't solve, and that was seldom.

"I'm a girl short, Mr. Lewis," she said. He regarded her neat, black dress and wondered how much she had paid for it. Lewis had that kind of mind. He was curious about everything. "Lana Evans hasn't come in."

"Oh? Is she ill?"

"I don't know, Mr. Lewis. I called her apartment an hour ago, but there was no answer. I must have another girl. Could I have Maria Wells from the general office?"

"Yes, of course. Tell her I hope she will help us out." Lewis smiled. "I think she will." Then he thought, looking at Rita inquiringly, "Odd about Lana. I can't remember her taking a night off without letting us know. You say she doesn't answer her phone?"

"That's right, Mr. Lewis."

Lewis shrugged.

"Well, try again later." He smiled, nodded and dismissed her. This was a domestic problem he knew she could handle. As she left him, he turned once again to survey the lower terrace, then satisfied that everything was working with its normal clockwork efficiency, he made his way through the big gambling hall.

At this hour only fifty or sixty habitués were at the roulette tables: elderly, rich residents of Paradise City who remained rooted to the tables from midday to midnight.

He caught the eye of one of the croupiers who had been in his service for the past eleven years. The man, fat, sleek, with bulging eyes, gave him a dignified nod as he guided a stack of chips with his rake to an old woman who reached out her little fat fingers to welcome them.

Lewis walked into the restaurant and had a word with Maître d'hôtel Giovanni whom he had stolen from the Savoy Hotel, London, at a considerable cost. There were a few early tourists, studying the enormous menus that a suave Captain of Waiters had presented to them. In another hour, the restaurant would be a maelstrom of hungry, noisy people.

"All well, Giovanni?" Lewis asked.

"Perfect, sir." The Maître d'hôtel lifted a supercilious eyebrow. The very suggestion that it couldn't be well in his restaurant was an implied insult.

Lewis studied the menu that Giovanni handed him. He nodded.

"Looks excellent. Tomorrow is the night. Anything special?"

"We have grouse and salmon from Scotland. Baby lamb from Normandy. The *plat de jour*—for the tourists—will be *coq au vin*. Monsieur Oliver of Paris is sending us by air his new dish . . . *lapin et lamproie*."

Lewis looked suitably impressed.

"So we won't starve?"

The tall, thin Maître d'hôtel flicked away an invisible speck of dust from his immaculate dinner jacket.

"No, sir. We won't starve."

Lewis moved through the restaurant, noticing that each table had a bowl of orchids cunningly lit from below. He thought Giovanni's table decoration excellent, but he wondered about the cost, for Harry Lewis was an extremely practical man.

Out on the terrace, amid the noise of the chatter and the soft music of the band, he paused until he caught the eye of the head barman. Fred, thickset, short, slightly ageing, moved towards his master, a happy grin on his fiery red face.

"Going to be a big night, sir," he said. "Can I get you a drink?"

"Not right now, Fred. Tomorrow is going to be the night."

"I guess. Well, we can take care of it."

Seeing flicking fingers across the terrace, Fred turned and hurried away.

Satisfied that his machine was working smoothly, Lewis returned to his office. He had still a number of letters to deal with before he had a simple meal served on his desk. He was unaware of Jess Chandler, sitting alone at the table away from the band, nursing a whisky and soda, watched him leave the terrace.

Chandler was uneasy. Maisky's plan seemed sound, but he was worried at the enormity of the task. Here, after spending an hour or so on the terrace, watching, seeing all these people, arrogant and so confident in their wealth, the steady movement of the guards, .45 revolvers at their hips, the feeling of solidarity that the Casino exuded, made Chandler realise that this was a millionaire's bastion that was protected alarmingly well, and that anyone planning a robbery was taking on more than a major operation.

He had no misgivings about his own part in the operation. He was quite happy with the role that Maisky had given him. It was just the right job for him. He was completely confident that he could talk his way into the vault. What really worried him was that Maisky had picked Jack Perry for the operation. Chandler knew all about Perry. This man wasn't human. In a squeeze, he wouldn't hesitate to kill, and violence to Chandler was something he had always avoided and feared. If Perry started a massacre—and he might well do—then they all were in real trouble. He knew Mish was a clever technician. He knew nothing about Wash nor did he care, but Perry scared him.

Suddenly sick of the luxury surrounding him, he paid his check and walked into the gambling rooms. For a moment he paused to look around, noting the four uniformed guards who stood by the box elevators that conveyed the money up and down to the vaults. They all looked young, aggressive and alert. Grimacing, he walked across the ornate lobby where he collected his passport from the Check-in office. There was a big crowd coming in: every woman wore diamonds and had a mink stole—the uniform of the rich. Chandler was aware that some of them looked at him with interest, their bored eyes lighting up. Not in the mood, he ignored them.

As he walked down the flat, broad steps into the garden of the Casino, he saw Jack Perry, wearing a tuxedo, a cigar between his teeth, coming towards him. Chandler turned away from the approaching man and made his way down a narrow path that led to the beach.

Maisky had told them all—not Wash, of course—to take a look at the Casino and to familiarise themselves with the background of the place. Now, Perry had arrived, but Chandler had no wish to be seen with him.

After walking down a long flight of steps, he found himself on the broad promenade that ran around the Casino's private bathing beach.

There were still a number of people in swim suits on the beach, some sitting at tables, drinking, others in the sea. He paused to watch a couple water-ski-ing, holding a flaming torch in their hands and both very expert. Then he continued on his way, leaving the Casino beach and taking the circular road that would eventually lead him back to his hired car which he had parked near the entrance to the Casino.

Out of the shadows, a girl came towards him. She wore a white dress with a frilly wide skirt, decorated with a rose pattern design. She was very tanned and exciting to look at. Her dark hair framed her face and hung to her shoulders. She carried a guitar in her hand.

Because she was different to the rich bitches of the Casino and also somehow vaguely familiar, Chandler paused and smiled at her. She stopped and regarded him. A cheap brooch of paste diamonds in her hair caught the overhead light and flashed.

"Hello, Jess . . ."

He stiffened, then quickly relaxed. He had no idea who she was. The trouble with me is, he thought wryly, there are too many women in my life. I know I've met her before, but who is she?

"Hello, baby," he said with his charming smile. "That's a beautiful body your dress is wearing."

She laughed.

"You said exactly that very thing two years ago when we met almost right on this spot . . . but you wouldn't remember."

Then he did remember. Two years ago he had come to Paradise City because a pal of his had the crazy idea of walking into the Casino with ten armed men and clearing the tables. He had quickly backed out of that plan and his pal, discouraged, had decided that maybe the idea wasn't all that hot.

Chandler had liked the City and had stayed on for a week. It was while he was wandering around the back of the Casino that he had met this girl. He even remembered her name. Lolita (that was one hell of a name now) Seravez. She came from Brazil and made a tricky living working the lesser-class restaurants, singing and playing her guitar. But Chandler had found her love technique stimulating and interesting. He had had no trouble about that. They had looked at each other, and there was a sudden fusion, and ten minutes later, they were holding each other on the hot sand, oblivious to anything except their lust.

"Hi . . . Lolita," he said. "This is the nicest moment of my life. Let's go somewhere where we can be alone."

"My Jess . . . the one-track mind." She regarded him affectionately. "What are you doing here?"

"Don't let's waste time talking about a thing like that." He hooked his arm in hers. "Let's go look at the sea and feel the sand. Baby . . . if you knew how glad I am to see you."

"I've got the idea," she said, going with him. "It's mutual. I'm glad to see you."

Washington Smith lit another cigarette. He was sitting by the open window of his small, airless cabin at the Welcome Motel. Maisky had warned him not to show himself until ten o'clock when he had a rendezvous at Maisky's bungalow. This, Wash accepted. No one wanted to see a shabbily dressed negro on the streets. Questions would be asked. The police would converge on him. People would stare at him in that contemptuous way only the rich whites can stare at a negro.

Mish Collins, stretched out on the bed, was examining the blueprints of the Casino's electrical wiring. He had come over in his hired car to collect Wash. They still had half an hour before they need leave for Maisky's bungalow.

"What are you going to do with your share, Mish?" Wash asked, turning away from the window.

Mish laid down the blueprint. He fed a cigarette to his lips and set fire to it.

"Well . . . three hundred thousand dollars! Yeah, it's a lump of money, isn't it? I've been making plans. I'm going to buy me a small boat. I've always wanted a boat. Nothing very elaborate, but big enough to live on. I'll find me a girl and then she and I will take a look at the Keys. I reckon that would be fun, just to keep sailing, stopping when I feel like it, changing the girl when I get bored with her, eating well. That's the life for me." He turned on his side so he could look at Wash. "How about you?"

"I've always wanted to be a doctor," Wash said. "I'll use some of the money to train. Then, with the rest of it, I'll buy a practice in New York."

"For Pete's sake!" Mish was startled. "Do you think you can make it?"

Wash nodded.

"Of course. Given the means, and if you make up your mind, there isn't anything a guy can't do."

"Yeah . . . but all that study! Jeepers! It wouldn't suit me. Don't you want a girl, Wash?"

"I want a wife and family, but that will have to wait." Wash let smoke drift down his flat nostrils. "Think we are going to get away with this, Mish?"

"Why, sure. Maisky is a real, bright boy. We'll get away with it . . . I promise you that. I wouldn't have brought you into it, Wash, if I hadn't been sure myself."

"It won't be as easy as he makes out."

"Well, okay, we can't expect it to be easy. You don't pick up three hundred thousand dollars without sweating a little."

"No."

Wash turned back to the window and Mish, after looking thoughtfully at him, picked up the blueprint, but now he found he couldn't concentrate. A doctor! he was thinking. This dinge certainly had big ideas. What the hell makes him imagine anyone would want to be treated by a little smoke like him?

Mish found himself growing resentful. He could understand a guy when he was in the money wanting a woman, a boat and lots to eat and drink, but this idea of becoming a doctor if he had money? he asked himself. That was the point. This was something that jarred his philosophy. He knew a doctor ran around all the time, never had any peace, got night calls, sat in a dreary office listening to people moaning about themselves—jerks who would be better off dead—what an ambition for anyone to have who owned three hundred thousand dollars!

He put down the blueprint and again looked at Wash as he sat staring out of the window. Then he shook his head and shrugged. Well, the hell with it! Why should he care?

Half an hour later, the two men got out of Mish's hired car, carrying a suitcase each and walked up the narrow path that led to Maisky's bungalow. A light showed through the curtains, and the door opened immediately when Mish thumbed the bell push.

Maisky waved them in.

"I hope everything so far is well," Maisky said as he led the way into the small, shabbily furnished sitting-room. Jack Perry was already there, lounging in the only comfortable chair in the room, a cigar burning evenly between his teeth. He nodded indifferently as the two men came in.

Maisky went over to the table on which stood a bottle of Scotch, glasses and a container of ice.

"Chandler is still to come," he said, "but we can start without him."

He made two drinks after Wash had shaken his head. Mish dropped his large body into a chair that creaked under his weight. He accepted the drink, then watched Maisky hand the other drink to Perry.

"I will ask you to try on your uniforms," Maisky said. "I think they will fit. I have taken trouble with them. Then we will go through the whole plan."

A ping on the doorbell made him break off. He went to the front door and returned with Chandler, a suitcase in hand.

Chandler came into the room, nodded to the other men, set down the suitcase and accepted a drink. Watching him, Maisky realised he had been with a woman. The relaxed, satiated expression on the handsome face was enough to tell Maisky this. It didn't worry him. He was confident enough in Chandler to know that he wouldn't talk, even to a woman.

"There is one thing that is important," Maisky said, sitting on the edge of the table, "which I forgot to mention last night. When Jess and Wash get into the vault, they will find the money is packaged in five, ten, twenty, one-hundred and five-hundred-dollar bills. You two will take only the five-hundred-dollar bills. There isn't a great deal of space in the carton and we want as much money as we can get. But you must also take as many five-dollar bills as you can carry in your pockets. On this money we will have to live for three or even six weeks. I am still not sure that the five-hundred-dollar bills aren't marked. So while the heat is on, we must only spend the five-dollar bills . . . understand?"

"Marked?" This from Mish. "You think they would mark their big bills?"

"I don't know. I doubt it, but we mustn't take any chances. Until the heat has cooled off, we will not spend one single five-hundred-dollar bill."

The four men nodded.

"Well, you all know the plan and you have had time to think it over. Have you any suggestions?" Maisky looked around, his head slightly on one side, his eyes probing.

"This cylinder of gas," Mish said. "I could fix a gimmick so that the gas was released when they open the carton. Would that help?"

"And what would happen to them? The gas operates in ten seconds." Maisky sounded a little impatient. "They must have their gas masks on before the gas is released."

Mish scratched his thick nose and shrugged.

"Yeah . . . well, it was an idea."

Chandler said, "Suppose we work through the whole plan? The timing has got to be exact. Why does Mish have to put the air conditioner on the blink?"

"If the temperature is too low, the gas isn't efficient. It will work, of course, but not so fast. It is essential that the room isn't cold."

"About the timing . . . aren't we cutting it fine if Mish starts operating at two-thirty?"

"That is right." Maisky slid off the table, went to a drawer and took out a sheet of paper. "I have revised the schedule. It's all here. You will each be given a copy. But before we go into that, I want you all to try on your uniforms."

Ten minutes later, Chandler, Perry and Wash had on the I.B.M. service uniforms and found no fault with them. Mish was wearing the Paradise City's Electricity Co's uniform.

"Yes, they will do very well," Maisky said after a careful inspecton. "Now, I will show you the truck."

"Just a second," Chandler said. "How did you get hold of these uniforms?"

Maisky regarded him, his gentle smile in evidence.

"You are very curious, my friend. I have many contacts. A tailor who owes me a lot was happy to make them . . . you need not worry. He won't talk."

"Who cares?" Mish said enthusiastically, regarding himself in the mirror on the wall. "They are great."

"Yes . . . the fit is good," Maisky said. "Now let me show you the truck."

He led them through the kitchen and into the double garage where a small truck was parked beside his Buick. On each of its sides was a bold painted sign: red letters against a white background. It read:

I.B.M.
THE BEST CALCULATORS IN THE WORLD.
WE DELIVER AND SERVICE AROUND THE CLOCK.

"You did this?" Mish asked, staring in obvious admiration.

"Yes . . . I think I can say there isn't much I can't turn my hand to," Maisky said, obviously pleased. "I have installed a gimmick on the dashboard so that with a lift of a lever, these signs can be jettisoned. We must not forget that once the robbery has been discovered, the truck will be red hot and we must get rid of these signs." He opened the double doors at the rear of the truck. Inside there was a long bench seat. "There will be room enough for you all to ride in the truck, except, of course, Mish, who will arrive and get away in his own car. There is also an arrangement by which I can change the number plates by another gimmick. The plates swivel over and new ones take their place." He demonstrated the changing of the plates while the four men watched, then with the air of a salesman, he said, "I have found a safe place, a mile from the Casino, where we will dump the truck. I will have my car there." He looked at Chandler, "I will ask you to follow me in your car tomorrow morning so that you can drive me back, after I have left my car. The sooner we get rid of the truck after we have the money, the better." He paused, looked at the four men, then asked politely, "Are there any questions?"

Chandler regarded the truck. He felt much more relaxed. The more he listened to this little man explain his plan, the more confident he became of success.

"What happens if we run into trouble at the Casino?" he asked. This was a question that was haunting him.

"What kind of trouble?" Maisky asked, raising his eyebrows. His calmness again added to Chandler's growing confidence. "I don't anticipate trouble."

"You can't say that . . . none of us knows," Chandler said sharply. "We might not get into the vault."

Maisky shrugged.

"In that case, we don't get the money . . . it's as simple as that. But I am sure you will get into the vault."

"What happens if we get the money and someone sets off the alarm?"

"No one will set off the alarm because Mish will have put it out of action."

Chandler moved uneasily. He was searching for trouble.

"Suppose some guard gets nosy?"

"Then Jack will take care of him."

There was a long pause, then Chandler said, "You mean he will kill the guard?"

"Listen, buddy-boy," Perry said in his soft, giggling voice, "don't worry your gut about what happens to who. You take care of your job . . . I'll take care of mine."

"We are going to make three hundred thousand dollars

each out of this operation," Maisky said. "You have to break eggs to make an omelette."

Chandler looked at Mish and Wash.

"Do you two want to get yourselves tied up in a murder rap?" he asked.

"Now, wait . . ." Maisky's voice was sharp. "I am satisfied that this operation will work. We don't have to consider violence. You are looking for trouble that doesn't exist."

"I don't want to be tied to a murder rap," Chandler said, and there was sweat on his face.

"Then what the hell are you here for?" Perry said. "Look, buddy-boy, be your age. Do your job and keep your worry gut of a mouth shut."

Again there was a pause, then Chandler, thinking of all that money, suddenly shrugged.

"So, okay . . . I keep my mouth shut . . ."

Mish said, now a little uneasy, "But suppose it does turn sour? Just what do we do?"

"It won't, but I agree with you, we should know what to do," Maisky said. "Whatever happens we come back here . . . if we have the money, we split it and go on our own ways . . . if we haven't got it, we still split up, but let us make this place here, which is quite safe, a meeting place after the operation."

Chandler hesitated, but he was now committed. He wasn't too happy, and he was scared of Perry, but the thought of all that money pushed him to agree.

"Okay . . . the uniforms are fine . . . the truck is fine . . . now let's look at the schedule."

Maisky smiled.

"Of course."

He led the way back into the bungalow.

three

THREE TIMES, during this hot Saturday morning, the telephone bell in Lana Evans' one room apartment rang continuously for several minutes. The nagging, persistent sound disturbed the Persian cat who still sat obstinately before the refrigerator, every now and then emitting a yowl of impatient indignation.

The first caller, around ten o'clock, was Terry Nicols, Lana's boy-friend. He listened to the steady, unanswered burr-burr-burr with exasperation. He knew Lana never got out of bed before ten. She couldn't still be sleeping with the telephone bell ringing like this! He wanted to make a date with her for Sunday night which was her night off. The two students who were his friends and who were waiting outside the telephone booth, kept showing him their wrist-watches through the dusty glass door. The time for the first morning's lecture was nearly due. With the exaggeration of youth, they began an elaborate countdown, and finally when they reached zero, they exploded into a pantomime of panic. Terry slammed down the receiver and raced with them across the corridor to the lecture room.

At eleven o'clock, Rita Watkins phoned from the Casino. She listened to the unanswered ring, then, frowning, a little worried, she replaced the receiver.

At one-thirty, Terry, munching a sandwich, again tried to contact Lana, then, failing again, he decided she must be on the beach, sunbathing. Irritated, he hung up. At little after two o'clock, Rita Watkins called again. Maria Wells hadn't been a success in the vault. This was understandable. The work was exacting and had to be done at high speed. Maria just hadn't the experience. Rita quailed at the thought of having her on this Saturday night when the pressure would be on. She just had to have Lana Evans back on the job.

What could have happened to the girl? she wondered as she replaced the receiver. She had a couple of hours to spare and she decided to drive over and find out for herself.

Mrs. Mavdick owned the apartment block. She was a large woman with jet-black dyed hair and an enormous floppy bosom which she held together under her soiled cotton wrap.

She regarded Rita's trim figure with disapproval. Those firm breasts, that flat stomach, the long shapely legs were to Mrs. Mavdick the symbols of sin.

"She's on the third floor," she said. "Seen her? No . . . I've things to do. I don't see people unless they come to see me. What's the excitement about?"

"There's no excitement. I have tried to contact her on the telephone . . . she doesn't answer."

Mrs. Mavdick thumped her floppy bosom. She had difficulty in breathing.

"Well, you don't have to answer the phone, do you?"

Rita climbed the stairs and rang Lana's front-door bell. She saw a bottle of milk and a copy of the *Paradise City Herald* by the door. She waited, rang again, then with a feeling of frustration, she descended the stairs.

Mrs. Mavdick was still propping her gross body against her door.

"She isn't there," Rita said.

Mrs. Mavdick smirked. Her long, yellow teeth made her look like a cunning horse.

"Well . . . we're only young once," she said, fighting for her breath. "Girls like boys . . . it's not my business . . . I never worry when my folk aren't at home."

Rita regarded her with disgust and then went out into the hot sunshine to her car.

Detective 2nd Grade Tom Lepski was considered to be the toughest officer attached to the Paradise City police force. He was tall, wiry, with a lined, sun-tanned hawklike face and ice-blue eyes. He was not only tough, he was also ambitious.

At seven o'clock, he strode into the station house wearing a sharp-looking tuxedo, a blood-red bow tie and his shoes were of black reverse calf.

Charlie Tanner gaped at him.

"Well, drop me down a well!" he exclaimed. "If it isn't our Tom, got up like a goddam movie star!"

Lepski adjusted his bow tie. There was a smirk of satisfaction on his lean face.

"What's wrong with being a movie star? Let me tell you something, Charlie . . . if Hollywood could see me now!"

Charlie Tanner pursed his thick lips and made a loud, rude noise. "If Hollywood saw you now, they would give up making movies. What's the big idea?"

"You ask the Chief . . . if he wants you to know, he will tell you . . . perhaps," and with a jaunty stride, Lepski went through the charge room and up the stairs to Terrell's office.

Here Terrell and Beigler regarded him, careful not to show their startled surprise.

"Reporting, sir," Lepski said, his lean face dead pan. "I'm taking four men to the Casino right away. Any orders, sir?"

Terrell's fleshy face creased into a grin.

"Does you credit, Tom. That's a nice outfit you've got there."

"Very fancy," Beigler said. "Do you own it or have you rented it?"

Lepski stiffened and Terrell said quickly, "Who cares? Okay, Tom, watch it. Are you wearing a gun?"

Lepski gave Beigler a sour look, then nodded.

"Yes, sir."

"Lewis seems to expect trouble. I don't know why, but keep circulating. There'll be a lot of money in the Casino tonight."

"I'll take care of it, sir."

"Okay. I'll be here until midnight. Joe will be here all night. If anything starts . . . I guess I don't have to tell you what to do."

Lepski nodded.

"I'll take care of it, sir."

"And listen, Tom," Beigler said, "just because you are wearing that monkey suit, don't imagine you are one of those rich slobs who are trying to enjoy themselves. Keep off drink and away from the girls. Get it?"

Lepski again nodded.

"Yes, Sergeant."

"And take that James Bond look off your face. You're a cop, and you have a job to do," Beigler said.

"Yes, Sergeant," Lepski said, his face dead pan.

"Okay, Tom," Terrell said. "Get off. I hope we won't be hearing from you."

"Yes, sir," Lepski said and walked out of the office. He stabbed a finger at the door when he had shut it, and then walked down to where Charlie Tanner was handing over to another sergeant.

Tanner said, "I bet Joe loved you, dressed up like that."

"He did," Lepski said. He shot his cuffs, flicked at his tie and, leaving Tanner gaping with admiration, he walked down to the waiting police car.

At midnight, Harry Lewis locked away the papers on his desk, lit a cigar, and left his office. His secretary had gone home a few minutes before. Now, he could concentrate on the activities in the gambling hall. He would remain, moving around on the first floor until three a.m., before going back to his luxury villa. He took the elevator down to the first floor.

So far, the evening had been uneventful. The gambling had begun at ten-thirty. Every fifteen minutes, Lewis received reports from the croupiers. As was expected, the gambling had been high and reckless. So far the Casino was ahead, but there was a syndicate of Brazilians who could be troublesome. Lewis decided it was time he went down and watched the play.

As he wandered into the gambling hall, he spotted Lepski, his alert ice-blue eyes surveying the scene.

Lewis went over to him.

"Glad you are here, Tom," he said, shaking hands. "How is Carroll?"

Carroll Mayhew was Lepski's *fiancée*. They were hoping to get married at the end of the year, and Lepski felt certain Lewis would donate a handsome wedding present.

"Fine, sir," he said. "No trouble there. No trouble here. These guys are certainly tossing their money around."

"Well . . . if you have, you toss it . . . if you haven't, you shouldn't," Lewis said and smiled. "Your men around?"

"On the terrace, sir. They have instructions to wander in every ten minutes. You wouldn't want a bunch of flat-feet in here all the time."

Lewis laughed.

"I'll leave it to you, Tom. Just keep an eye on the money," and nodding he walked on.

There's a guy, Lepski thought. A real, nice, regular guy. He straightened his bow tie which was worrying him, then he went out on to the terrace where his four patrolmen were standing watchfully in obscure corners.

He wasn't to know he was wasting their and his time. When the attack was to come, it would come in the soft underbelly of the Casino—in the vault where no police officer was on guard.

The money passing across the green-baize tables was as nothing compared to the money steadily piling up in the vault. The gamblers were having a bad night. The money was flowing into the Casino's vault . . . thousands and thousands of dollars.

In the cool atmosphere of the vault Rita Watkins directed the operation of handling the in-and-out flow of the money.

The girls fed the stacks of money as the money came from the elevators into an electronic device that automatically sorted the bills into their various denominations. The machine then counted them, clocking the total on a calculator. The bills were then paper-banded in fifty lots by the machine and were fed through a slot where two other girls piled the banded money in its various denominations on a rack.

Money came in: money went out. When a red light flashed under a number on Rita's desk, she directed more money to be sent up in the elevator, noting the number of the table in the gambling hall that had called for more supplies. The work was fast and non-stop, and no girl could afford to fumble.

Watching them, seated on stools, either side of the steel door of the vault, were two armed guards.

One of them, a tall, rangy youth whose name was Hank Jefferson, was bored to tears with his job. He thought if he had to sit on this stool, watching all that money for another few weeks, he would go screwy. He was planning to put in for a transfer. Even walking around the outside of the Casino endlessly was better than sitting in this vault just staring at thousands of dollars.

The other guard, an older man, heavily built and slightly balding, was Bic Lawdry. He had the mind of a vegetable and was happy enough to watch the girls, studying their trim bodies, dreaming erotic dreams as he picked his teeth with a match end, satisfied that he had the softest job in the world.

Beyond the steel door was a long passage that led to the Staff entrance to the Casino. At the door that led to the rear of the Casino and to a broad strip of tarmac where trucks arrived each morning delivering food, drink, cigarettes and other provisions for the restaurant, was a doorman.

Sid Regan, the doorman, was sixty-one years of age. In another four years he would have to retire. He had worked at the Casino for thirty-eight years. He was short, fat and bulky with an amiable, freckled face, thinning, greyish hair and small, humorous eyes. Regan loved his job. He regretted he was slowly but inevitably reaching the age when he would no longer work at the Casino. He was what is known as a character. This, perhaps, was kind. The younger members of the staff called him a goddam, yakiting, old bore.

The trouble with Regan was he had too many memories. He couldn't resist talking about the good old days. Few bothered to listen to him, but this didn't discourage him. He always managed to find some unwary person who, trapped by his guile, had to stand impatiently while he described with a wealth of detail the glories of the past.

This bulky, elderly man, who did his job well, who had given years of faithful service, represented Harry Lewis's most serious mistake with his staff. Regan had a very important job: to see no one should ever pass his glass box without being known or without he being absolutely sure of their credentials. Regan was proud of his responsibility, and this Maisky had discovered. Maisky had found out by listening to gossip that Regan liked to act on his own initiative. He disliked being told anything. He had held his job successfully for years . . . he wasn't a kid. Why should he be told what to do? Maisky was gambling on this attitude of Regan's, and it was a successful gamble.

When Regan saw a small truck with the well-known I.B.M. letters painted on its sides pull up at the Staff entrance, he was puzzled, but not suspicious. He decided that something had gone wrong and Head Office had failed to alert him. He was thinking, as Jess Chandler got out of the truck, that those girls in the office were getting more and more inefficient.

Chandler had been well coached by Maisky. He walked up to the glass box, pushed his peaked cap to the back of his head and nodded to Regan.

"You have a breakdown in the vault," he said. "My goddam luck! I was right in the middle of a musical on the Telly when the call came through. What a time!" He handed a delivery note to Regan. "Let's snap it up, mister. You know about it, don't you?"

Maisky had impressed on Chandler to use this phrase. He had watched Regan as he had walked to and fro from the Casino to his home. He had seen him stop and talk to people and had seen their desperately bored expressions. He had come to the correct conclusion that Regan imagined that he was the Casino, and he felt certain that Regan would never admit to not knowing about such an important event as a calculator having broken down in the vault.

But his guess hung on a knife's edge. For a split second, Regan was in two minds whether to call the office for confirmation, then, knowing the office was shut and feeling hurt that no one had bothered to consult him, he accepted the delivery note, shifted his glasses to the end of his nose and studied it. This was in order. It had taken Maisky some days to get a printed form from I.B.M.'s local office, but he had got it.

"Yeah . . . yeah," Regan said, pushing up his glasses and regarding Chandler. "I know all about it. They are waiting for you, boy. You take it right in," and he banged down the rubber stamp on the delivery note: a stamp that cleared anyone walking into the forbidden territory.

Wash now appeared from out of the truck, and a moment later, Perry appeared. While Wash and Chandler manhandled the big carton out of the truck, Perry strolled over to Regan's glass box.

"Hi, pal," he said, feeding a cigarette between his thin lips. "Are you the guy who had his photo in the paper last week?"

This again was information supplied by Maisky who had told Perry to use it.

Regan preened himself, taking off his glasses.

"That was me. You see it? Mind you, it's an old picture, but I reckon I don't change much. I've been in this box for thirty-eight years. Imagine! You can understand why they put my photo in the paper, can't you?"

"Is that right?" Perry's fat face showed impressed astonishment. "Thirty-eight years! For Pete's sake! I've only lived in this City for three years. I bet you've seen a lot of changes, mister."

Again this was Maisky's dialogue. Regan snapped at it as a trout snaps at a fly.

By now Chandler and Wash were past him and walking down the narrow corridor, carrying the carton.

"Changes?" Regan said, accepting the cigarette Perry offered him. "You bet. I remember . . ."

Outside, sitting in the truck, his clawlike hands gripping the steering wheel, Maisky waited.

Twenty-five minutes before the truck arrived at the Staff entrance, Mish Collins drove up to the Casino in his hired car, swung a tool box over his shoulder by its leather strap, got out and stared up at the lighted entrance.

The doorman, magnificent in his bottle-green and cream uniform, converged on him. The doorman considered this big, fat man in uniform was spoiling the de luxe background of the Casino.

Before he could remonstrate, Mish gave him a friendly grin and said, "You have an emergency. Mr. Lewis flashed us. Seems you have a circuit breakdown somewhere."

The doorman stared at him.

"I haven't heard about it," he said. He had been with the Casino almost as long as Regan. He had collected a fortune in tips by opening and shutting car doors. During the years of standing in the hot sunshine, doing a simple, mechanical job, he had become alarmingly slow witted.

"Look, chum," Mish said, his voice suddenly sharp, "do I have to worry about that? This is an emergency. It's no skin off my snout if the electricity fails, but I've got this call and whoever made the call is laying eggs. Where do I find the fuse boxes?"

The doorman blinked, then suddenly realised what it would mean if the Casino was without electricity. He broke out in a cold sweat.

"Sure . . . I'll show you . . . you come with me."

Mish had almost to run to keep up with him as he led him down a narrow alley, lined on either side by orange trees, heavy with fruit, and to a steel door, set in a wall."

The doorman produced a key and unlocked the door.

"There you are," he said, snapping on the light. "What's wrong?"

"How do I know, pal?" Mish said, setting down his tool box. "I'll have to take a look, won't I? You want to stay and watch?"

The doorman hesitated. Somewhere at the back of his turgid mind he vaguely remembered the rules of the Casino: no one should be allowed into the control room without authorisation and should never be left alone there. But this was only the vaguest memory. He thought of the people still arriving at the Casino, even at this late hour, and the dollar tips he was missing. He eyed Mish's uniform and the tool box with *Paradise City Electricity Corp*. written on the lid in startling white letters.

What was he worrying about? he thought. He should be on his job.

"You fix it," he said. "I'll be back in ten minutes."

"Don't rush," Mish said. "I'll be here for at least half an hour."

"Well, okay, but you wait here. Don't go away until I get back." The doorman hurried away up the path.

Mish grinned. He turned to examine the fuse boxes. He quickly found the fuse that controlled the calculator. He had some minutes yet before he went into action. He lit a cigarette and then opened the tool box.

He was very calm and sure of success.

Bic Lawdry felt a drop of sweat roll down his nose and then drop on his hand. He had been dozing and, surprised, he stiffened, now aware of the heat in the vault. His fat face creased into a puzzled frown.

"Hey! Ain't it getting hot in here?" he demanded, leaning over to give Hank Jefferson a shove. Hank was absorbed in a paperback with a jacket picture of a naked girl lying in a pool of blood.

"Wrap up!" Hank said. "I'm busy."

Bic wiped the sweat off his nose and glared at the air conditioner. He slid off his stool and walked over to the machine, putting his hand against the grille. Only hot, steamy air was being forced out by the fan.

"The goddam thing's broken down," he announced.

The four girls were working at high pressure. The tide was now turning, and the gamblers had at last hit a winning streak.

Rita, busy answering the red flashes on her desk, felt her dress sticking to her, but she couldn't stop. The activity and the need for concentration allowed her only to wave her hand, signalling to Bic to do something about the breakdown.

Such was Bic's nature, he looked helplessly at Hank. If he could find someone to take action on any little thing, he inevitably passed the buck.

"Hank! Quit that muck! The air conditioner has packed up!"

Hank dragged his eyes away from the small print. Right now, a girl was being raped. She was putting up a terrific fight and the lurid details intrigued him. He considered Bic dumb and lazy, and he had no patience with him.

"Drop dead!" he said. "*You* do something about it for a change." Then he returned to his reading.

There came a sharp rap on the door, and at the same time the whining sound from the calculator slowed, then suddenly ceased.

"Damn!" Rita exclaimed. "Now the calculator has stopped!"

The four girls paused. They suddenly realised how warm the vault was growing. The piles of money, some banded, some only half-way through the counting machine, now lay in inert piles.

Again the rap sounded on the door.

With a sigh of exasperation, Hank got off his stool, shoved his paperback into his hip pocket and opened the grilled, judas window. He saw a tall, good-looking man, wearing a peak cap with the yellow and black I.B.M. badge on it, regarding him.

"Yeah?"

"Delivering a calculator," Chandler said briskly. "You've got trouble, haven't you?"

Hank stared at him, his alert mind immediately suspicious.

"You psychic or something? It's only just this moment broken down."

"Had a call from Mr. Lewis," Chandler said and shoved the delivery note through the judas window.

Rita came over and took the delivery note from Hank. She saw Regan's stamp on it and that was enough for her.

"For heaven's sake! Let them in! Let's get this thing working again," she said, then rushed back to her desk where the red lights were flashing.

Hank unlocked the door.

"Okay . . . come on in."

The heat in the room had risen sharply.

"Miss Watkins," one of the girls complained, "can't we get something done? It's so hot here . . ."

"All right . . . all right," Rita snapped. "Give me a minute . . ."

Chandler and Wash were now in the vault. They set down the big carton on a desk. As they did so, Mish, with excellent split-second timing, replaced the fuse to the air conditioner. With a protesting growl, the machine started up again.

"There you are," Rita said, waving her hands. "It's on again."

Chandler, very tense, but his hands steady, half lifted the lid of the carton. Maisky had made it easy for him. The lid lifted easily. As he slid his hand into the carton, groping for a gun, Hank moved over, a puzzled, suspicious expression on his lean face.

Bic had already returned to his stool. Now the air conditioner was working, he was happy to return to his dreams.

Wash stepped forward, blocking Hank off, his back to him. He was having difficulty in breathing. Sweat dripped down his black face.

Chandler's hand found the gun. He whipped it out of the carton, then took a quick step away from the desk. Well rehearsed, Wash leaned forward, getting out of Chandler's range of fire. He reached into the carton, grabbed up a gas mask and with shaking hands, put it on.

Chandler was yelling, "None of you move! This is a stick-up. Hear me? None of you move!"

Hank froze, his eyes widened as Wash, now with his gas mask on, whirled around, gun in hand. Bic sat motionless on his stool, his fat face stricken with alarm. Very slowly, he raised his hands above his head.

Rita, calm, slid her foot towards the hidden alarm button under her desk. She found and pressed it, not knowing that ten minutes before the raid, Mish had removed the fuse that controlled the alarm system.

Swearing under his breath, Chandler had trouble in getting his mask on, but he got it on finally while the two guards were threatened by Wash's gun. Then Chandler rapped the head of the gas cylinder hard on the desk.

The result startled him. The cylinder seemed to jump in his hand. A cloud of white vapour suddenly filled the room. Dropping the cylinder, Chandler started back.

Maisky had told him the gas would operate in ten seconds. He hadn't believed this was possible. Hank was standing right in the middle of the cloud as it exploded out of the cylinder. He went down as if his legs had become boneless, slamming against Chandler and sending him staggering.

Rita Watkins, also near the congestion of gas, went next. Her hand started to her throat, but failed to complete the journey. She spread across her desk, her skirts riding up over her thighs, her long hair cascading into a wastepaper basket full of discarded memos.

The other girls collapsed almost simultaneously. The

last to go was Bic Lawdry. With bulging eyes and a limp hand groping for his .45, he struggled off the stool, then his legs gave way and he crashed down on the floor at Wash's feet.

Chandler stood for a long moment staring through the goggles of his mask, feeling sick and frightened, then seeing Wash was already taking up handfuls of neatly packed $500 bills, he pulled himself together and joined him.

Working like madmen, they quickly filled the carton. Even in his panic, Chandler realised that Wash was much calmer than he was. The negro was stacking the bills fast, but with care, using every available inch of space in the carton.

Seven minutes later, the carton was full. Chandler replaced the lid.

"Come on . . . let's get out of here!" he said, his voice muffled, his face, under the mask, streaming with sweat.

Wash motioned to the rack containing the $5 bills. Chandler had forgotten Maisky's instructions. He ran to the rack and taking several bundles of money, wedged them into his hip pockets and in the pockets of his blouse. Wash followed his example.

Unable to carry more, the two men looked at each other and nodded.

They were aware of three blinking red lights on Rita's desk. Chandler was aware too of Rita's long legs and her white thighs as she sprawled across the desk.

They caught hold of the carton, startled by its weight, then, opening the steel door, they edged out into the passage.

By this time the air conditioner had cleared the gas, and they paused to rip off their gas masks.

Fifteen yards down the passage, Perry, his broad back blocking Regan's view of the vault door, continued to listen to the old man's story of a gambler who, having lost all his money, had offered his mistress on the next spin of the wheel.

"With his luck running so bad," Regan said, grinning,

"I'd have taken the bet. She was quite a chick. Mind you, I like 'em built big, and this chick was the original feather bed." He shook his head. "They threw him out and the chick as well . . . a darn shame."

Leaving the gas masks on the floor, Chandler and Wash, Wash walking backwards, moved down the corridor, carrying the carton.

Perry glanced over his shoulder.

"Well, I guess the boys have fixed it," he said. "Glad to have talked to you, mister . . . a privilege. You sure have been interesting. I'll get the truck open."

He walked into the hot, still night and opened the truck.

Maisky, dying little deaths, heard the doors open. He started the car's engine.

Regan adjusted his spectacles and looked at Chandler as he and Wash moved past him.

"Taking the old one away . . . it's snarled up," Chandler said, sweating under the load. "They're happy now . . . so long, mister."

Regan nodded.

"So long, boy."

At this moment Mike O'Brien, the top security guard of the Casino, decided to look in at the vault. This he did every three hours, and this was to be his last visit.

He arrived out of the darkness as Chandler and Wash were loading the carton into the truck.

Maisky, sitting motionless behind the steering wheel, saw him coming, but there was nothing he could do about it. He had no means of warning the other men that a guard was approaching.

Chandler had shut one of the truck doors and was shutting the other when he felt, rather than saw, Perry stiffen.

The next second he found himself confronted by a solidly built, middle-aged man wearing the uniform of the Casino's security guards, his level, dark eyes regarding him with a hard scrutiny.

"What's going on?" O'Brien demanded.

Chandler was vaguely aware that Perry had melted into

the shadows. He saw Wash, out of the corner of his eyes, take a slow step back.

Chandler was professional enough to realise this moment was his. This was the reason why Maisky had chosen him. This was why he would earn three hundred thousand dollars.

Keeping his face dead pan, his eyes slightly surprised, Chandler said, "Emergency, pal. We've just changed the calculator in the vault." He was a little uneasy to hear his voice sounded so husky. "Mr. Lewis's orders." He slammed the other door of the truck. "My luck! What a time to have an emergency."

"Hold it!" O'Brien snapped. "Open up. I want to look in the truck."

Chandler stared fixedly at him.

"Know something, pal? I want to get home. But okay, take a look," and he opened one of the truck doors.

O'Brien peered into the dark truck.

"What's in that box?"

"The calculator . . . the one that's broken down," Chandler said, now aware that he was beginning to sweat.

"You got a pass-out?" O'Brien asked.

"Why, sure . . . old man river gave it to us," Chandler said and jerked his thumb towards the glass box where Regan was watching what was going on.

"I want to see what's inside that box," O'Brien said. "Open it up."

Perry, listening, eased out his Colt .38. To the short barrel there was screwed a four-inch silencer.

Chandler felt sick. This was about to become the moment of violence he had been dreading, but without hesitation, he pulled the carton towards the end of the truck.

O'Brien moved forward. His broad back was turned to Perry. Wash, watching, felt his heart constrict. This fool! he was thinking. This conscientious fool! If he could only let the truck go!

Listening to all this, Maisky put the clutch out and gently moved into gear.

Perry lifted his gun and squeezed the trigger as O'Brien reached forward to open the carton.

The .38 slug smashed through O'Brien's rib cage and cut his heart in two. The sound of the gun was no more than the sharp clap of hands.

O'Brien fell forward as Maisky released the clutch and sent the truck shooting forward.

For a brief moment Perry remained motionless . . . a wisp of smoke drifting from his silencer, then he jerked up the gun and fired once more. The slug smashed through the door of the truck that had swung shut as the truck shot forward.

For a paralysed moment, Sid Regan watched his old friend O'Brien as he fell, then with a reaction astonishing for a man of his age, his hand slid under his desk to where a .45 revolver had lain, gathering the rust, for several years: a gun O'Brien had given him and which Regan had treated as a joke. His horny fingers found the trigger, hooked around it and pulled with violence. The gun in the confined space went off with a nerve-shattering bang, the bullet ploughing through the wooden partition of Regan's box and whistling past Chandler so close that he felt the wind of it against his face.

As Regan fired, he rolled off his stool and out of sight behind the wooden partition.

Perry swivelled around, lifting his gun, but Chandler's tense voice halted his murderous impulse.

"Get out! Quick!" Chandler cried and, turning, he ran up the alley.

Realising in seconds he would have a mass of guards converging on the entrance to the vault, Perry followed him.

Wash, shaking with shock, moved out of the shadows and bent over O'Brien. His first thought was to see if he could help the murdered man. He turned him over. The light from the doorway fell directly on O'Brien's dead face and, shuddering, Wash straightened. This was no one he could help. He looked to right and left, hesitating. His legs were shaky. There seemed no other way of escape except up the narrow, orange-tree-lined alley. As he stared up it, Tom Lepski, gun in hand, came swiftly down. Wash stopped, hesitated, unaware he held his gun in his hand, then in a moment of panic, he plunged towards Lepski.

Lepski's gun banged once and Wash was thrown backwards. He felt a burning sensation in his chest then the stars and the big floating moon dimmed into slow, empty darkness.

Sergeant Joe Beigler suppressed a yawn, then reached for a carton of coffee that stood on his desk. He poured coffee into a paper cup, then lit a cigarette. He looked around the dimly lit Detectives' room. The only other officer on duty was Detective 3rd Grade Max Jacoby who was crouched over a desk, reading a book.

"What the hell are you reading?" Beigler asked. He never read anything and resented those who did.

Jacoby, the keenest officer in the City's police force, young, Jewish and good looking, glanced up.

"Assimil . . ."

Beigler blinked at him.

"Assy . . . who?"

Patiently, Jacoby explained. "It's a French course. I'm trying to learn French, Sergeant."

"French?" Beigler sat back, astounded. "What the hell for?"

"Why do you learn anything?" Jacoby asked.

Beigler considered this, then he scratched his head.

"But French . . . for Pete's sake!" Beigler's fleshy face suddenly brightened. "You reckon on going to Paris, Max?"

"I don't know. Anything's possible."

"You want to parlez with the girls . . . that it?"

Jacoby controlled a sigh.

"That's it, Sarg," he said, glad not to explain that he wanted to better himself.

"Listen, son, I've been to Paris," Beigler said seriously.

"You don't have to talk French. If you want a girl, you just whistle. It's that easy. Rest your brains . . . you'll need them for your job."

"Yes, Sarg," Jacoby said and went back to the adventures of Monsieur Dupont who was ordering a coffee and making a tremendous fuss with the waiter.

At this moment, the telephone bell on Beigler's desk shrilled. Beigler scooped up the receiver with a large, hairy hand and listened to the voice that hammered against his ear drum, then he said, "Stay with it, Tom. I'll get Hess to you," and he slammed down the receiver. As he began to dial, he said without looking at Jacoby, "Call the Chief, Max. Robbery at the Casino. Two men dead," and then as Jacoby dropped his textbook and grabbed at another telephone, Beigler was already speaking to the Headquarters Control Room. "Alert all check points . . . robbery and murder at the Casino. All cars to be searched. Warning . . . these men are dangerous. Road blocks on all major and minor roads. They haven't been gone more than three minutes. Immediate action. Alert Hess." He waited only to hear the quiet, efficient voice of the controller say, "Okay, Sarg," and then he hung up.

He swivelled around in his chair and looked at Jacoby, who was just replacing his receiver.

"The Chief's coming," Jacoby said.

"Okay, Max. You stay here. I'm going down to the Casino." Beigler once again lifted the receiver. "Hess on duty?" he asked when the acting desk sergeant answered.

"Yeah. He's across the road, having a beer."

Beigler hung up, checked to see he was carrying his gun, then, struggling into his jacket, he left the Detectives' room, taking the stairs three at a time.

four

CHIEF OF POLICE TERRELL arrived at the Casino twenty minutes after the shooting. This was pretty fast going considering he had been in bed and asleep when Jacoby had called him.

Already the Homicide Squad, under Frank Hess, was at work. Dr. Lowis, the police surgeon, with two other doctors who had been in the Casino and had come to his aid, were working on the four unconscious girls and the two guards. The bodies of Mike O'Brien and Washington Smith were being photographed. Sergeant Beigler was trying to cope with Sid Regan. The old man was still in shock, but that didn't stop him from being garrulous. What he was saying was so mixed up, Beigler had trouble in controlling his temper.

Five cars, packed with patrolmen, had arrived, and the officers were now holding back a vast crowd of people, all anxious to get a glimpse of the bodies.

Harry Lewis, white-faced but calm, greeted Terrell as he slid out of his car.

"They've got away with nearly all our cash," Lewis said. "It's a disaster, Frank. We'll have to close the Casino tomorrow."

"They may have got your cash, Harry," Terrell said quietly, "but they haven't got away . . . yet. Let me get into the picture. You take it easy," and he walked over to Lepski, who was waiting for him. "What happened, Tom?"

Briefly, Lepski told him. He had heard a shot, rushed down to the vault, met the negro, who had shown fight, so Lepski had shot him.

While Terrell was listening to Lepski's report, Beigler spotted his Chief. He said to Regan, "Okay, you relax. I'll be right back. Just stay where you are," and he hurried over to Terrell.

"Well, Joe?"

"The old guy has seen them all, but he is in shock," Beigler said. "We'll have to be patient with him, Chief. Once he has got his balance, he should be able to give us a description of all the men involved. Seems there were three of them, plus the driver of the truck, who seems to have lost his nerve or else he ratted on his pals. As soon as O'Brien started trouble, the driver took off in the truck. At least the old man has given me a description of the truck and the licence number. I've already alerted the road patrols. The truck can't get far. It hasn't a chance of getting past the road blocks."

Terrell nodded. He was thankful he had a crew he could completely rely on.

"You keep working on him, Joe. We must have a description of all the men as soon as we can and then we will get the descriptions on the air. Watch him . . . he could be our star witness. See he's protected."

"Yes, Chief."

As Beigler went back to Regan, Terrell walked down the passage to the vault.

Dr. Lowis was standing by the unconscious bodies of the four girls laid out on the floor. The other two doctors were working anxiously on Hank Jefferson. Bic Lawdry was already showing signs of coming to life.

"Well, doc?" Terrell asked, pausing in the doorway.

"The girls will be all right," Lowis said. "It was some kind of paralysing gas. The container is on the floor over there. I haven't touched it. This chap . . ." He indicated Hank, "is in a pretty bad way. He must have had a heavy dose. The other guard will be all right."

Terrell's keen eyes moved around the vault. He took a plastic bag from his pocket and very carefully rolled the empty gas cylinder into it, then he sealed the bag as Harry Lewis came in.

"My doorman tells me that a Corporation electrician was in the control room without authorisation," he said. "He tells me the man reported a breakdown . . . there wasn't one. He must have been one of the gang."

"I'll talk to him," Terrell said. "How was it he didn't report to you?"

"It would seem my staff are having it too good," Lewis said, a bite in his voice. "This is going to cost him his job. I'll take you to him."

Beigler was talking to Sid Regan again.

"Let's skip the background build-up," he said impatiently. "What I want to know . . ." He paused as Lewis and Terrell came up the passage. "This old guy is driving me nuts," he said to Terrell. "I just can't keep him on the beam."

"Let me handle him," Lewis said quietly. He walked over to Regan who was sitting in his glass box, his eyes blank, but still talking. "Sid!" The firm voice made Regan lift his head. "You did a fine job," Lewis went on, putting his hand on the old man's arm. "Thanks . . . now, you can help the police find these men. They want a description of them. I know your photographic memory, Sid . . . no one like you to remember details . . . just think for a moment. There were three of them . . . is that right?"

The blankness went out of Regan's eyes. He nodded.

"You're right, Mr. Lewis. I remember them," and then

he began to talk sense, so fast, Beigler, notebook in hand, had difficulty in keeping up with him. "There was this short, fat guy with snow-white hair . . . he had a tattoo mark on his left hand . . . no, I'm wrong . . . it was his right hand . . . a girl with her legs apart. I've seen that before . . . you close your fist and her legs close. He was grinning all the time . . . blue eyes . . . then there was . . ."

"Keep talking, Sid, I'll be right back," Lewis said, patted the old man's shoulder, then, jerking his head at Terrell, he led the way out into the hot, still night.

Once clear of the Casino, Maisky slowed the speed of the truck, but he still maintained a steady forty miles an hour. He knew all the side roads that led eventually to the sea: a honeycomb of narrow lanes which he had studied now for months. He drove a hundred yards or so along the broad highway that led to Miami, then turned off down a narrow road. Once away from the highway, he flicked up the lever on his dashboard and the two I.B.M. signs dropped off the truck, banging down on the road. Slightly accelerating, he continued on down the road for the best part of a mile, then he turned left, and driving more slowly, he went down a narrow road, lined either side by luxury villas; another left turn brought him to the sea.

His plan was working out exactly as he had foreseen. He had been certain that trouble would start at the Casino. He had known O'Brien would be the explosive spark to start the trouble for he had watched the security guard night after night and had known to the minute when he would visit the vault. This was the only reason why he had included Jack Perry among the members of the gang. He wanted Perry to start trouble. It would then give him the chance of driving away and leaving the rest of them on their own. It had been like looking in a crystal ball . . . the events predicted . . . the events taking place.

His heart beat a little faster when he thought what might have happened if his planning had been wrong. But it hadn't been wrong, and now he was on the second leg of his operation to own two million dollars without having to share a dollar of it.

He drove the truck down on to the firm sand of the lonely beach where he had left his Buick. Speed was essential, he kept reminding himself, aware that his breathing was too fast and that he was sweating. There wasn't a second to waste.

Chandler knew of this hiding place. He had gone with Maisky that morning so that he could drive Maisky back after Maisky had left the Buick. There was a remote chance that Chandler would get away, find transport and come down to the hiding place. He might just possibly arrive at any moment.

Maisky manoeuvred the truck so that its rear bumper was close to the Buick's rear bumper. He slid out of the truck, ran around to the back of the truck and swung open the double doors. The light from the moon was sufficient for him to see the carton containing the money he had plotted to own for so many, long careful months. He leaned into the truck, caught hold of the carton and attempted to pull it towards him.

The carton remained motionless as if bolted to the floor. Its unexpected weight sent a surge of alarm through Maisky. He hadn't anticipated the carton could possibly be so heavy. Again he heaved his puny strength against the dead weight. The carton shifted a few inches and then again became immovable.

Maisky paused. Sweat was streaming down his thin face and he was shaking. The night was stiflingly hot. In the far distance, he could see people still enjoying themselves on the beach, some in the sea, others playing ball in the moonlight. There was a sudden, alarming stab of pain in his chest, and, with a feeling of dread, he realised the carton was too heavy for him to manhandle into the boot of the Buick.

Maisky was a man who never panicked, but at this moment, he had to make a stern effort to control himself as he was forced to accept the bitter truth that his age and his health weren't up to coping with this carton of money. To increase the pressure of panic, there was this possibility that Chandler or worse—Perry—might suddenly arrive.

He climbed into the truck and took the lid off the carton. No wonder it was so heavy! For a long moment, he squatted on his thin haunches, staring at the packets and packets of $500 bills. Then, working feverishly, he began to toss the packets into the open boot of the Buick. As he worked, feeling choked and hot in the stifling truck, he became more and more aware of the laughter and shouts of the people not more than eight hundred yards from him, enjoying themselves in the moonlight.

Every now and then, he paused to look along the deserted beach to his left . . . it was from this direction that either Chandler or Perry or both would come.

Finally, with an effort that exhausted him, he emptied half the carton, then scrambling out of the truck, he dragged the carton, that was still almost too heavy for him to handle, from the truck into the boot of the Buick. He then had to replace all the packets of money back into the carton before he could shut the door. One packet of money dropped in the sand. The paper band broke and a sudden, unexpected breeze sent some of the $500 bills careering towards the sea.

Such was Maisky's greed that he began to chase the bills, but, realising the danger of wasting more time, he slammed shut the boot, slid under the steering wheel and switched on the ignition. He pressed down on the accelerator. The engine gave a cough, but failed to start.

Maisky sat rigid, his hands gripping the wheel, sweat blinding him. Cautiously, he again pressed down on the accelerator. The engine kicked, whined and then was silent.

For several seconds, Maisky cursed vilely. He had been out of his mind to have tried to save money buying a secondhand car! He remembered another occasion of no importance when he had tried to start the car and had had trouble . . . so much trouble that he had had to telephone a breakdown garage to come out and start the car. But now there was no telephone, no breakdown garage and he was in trouble with this sonofabitch car. Once again he tried, and once again the engine failed to start.

He turned off the ignition, opened the glove compartment and took out a .25 automatic. He slid the gun into his jacket pocket, then he opened the engine cover. He peered into the dark interior. His heart was slamming against his ribs alarmingly and his breathing was coming in short, jerky bursts.

Cursing, he went to one of the sidepockets of the car, took out a flashlight and returned to the engine. He peered at the mass of wiring which meant nothing to him. He jerked at one or two of the cables in the hope that one of them had come loose, but he only succeeded in burning his hand on the hot cylinder head and getting black grease on his shirt cuff.

"You got trouble?"

The sound of a man's voice just behind him sent such a stab of alarm through Maisky's frail body that he thought he was about to have a heart attack. He leaned against the wing of the car, cold, shocked with fear, as the voice went on, "Could be oiled up, you know. It's the heat."

Very slowly, Maisky turned.

A young man . . . not more than eighteen or nineteen, wearing only a bathing slip, his tall body so deeply suntanned, he looked almost black in the moonlight, was standing close to him.

"I guess I startled you," the young man went on. "Sorry. I saw you trying to start her . . . I'm pretty good with cars."

Maisky was aware that the moonlight was falling directly on him. This young man with his young eyes and his young memory would be able to give the police a dangerous description of him. This was something Maisky had planned all along must never happen.

"You . . . are . . . very . . . kind," he said slowly, trying to control his breathing, trying desperately not to alert this young man that he was terrified. "Perhaps you could see what is wrong." He offered the flashlight.

He felt the warm, firm flesh as their hands met. The young man took the flashlight.

Maisky stepped back. He glanced again up the beach, aware of the passing minutes, aware that Chandler, Perry or even the police might arrive at any moment. He was also aware of three $500 bills lying in the sand close to the young man's feet. His hand crept to his jacket pocket. He drew the .25 gun and snicked back the safety catch. He held the gun down by his side.

"Your points are dirty," the young man said. "Have you a rag?"

With his left hand, Maisky gave him his handkerchief.

"Use that . . . it doesn't matter." He was surprised to hear how shaky his voice sounded.

The young man worked for several minutes, then stepped back.

"Try her now."

"Perhaps you would," Maisky said, moving away from the car.

The young man slid under the steering wheel, turned on the ignition and pressed down on the accelerator.

The engine fired immediately and Maisky drew in a sharp breath. For a long moment, he hesitated, then he remembered Lana Evans. He had killed her. One more death now didn't matter.

"It's okay," the young man said as he got out of the car. He suddenly stared down at his feet, seeing the three $500 bills in the sand. "Hey! Are these yours?"

As he bent to pick up the bills, Maisky took a quick step back, then aiming his gun at the young man's bent head, he squeezed the trigger.

Mish Collins was shutting the lid of his tool box when he heard the distant sound of a gunshot. He straightened, a red light flashing in his mind.

That meant trouble! In a few minutes, the place would

be swarming with police and security guards. He snapped off the light in the control room, then, leaving the tool box, he began to walk quickly up the narrow alley. Then he heard another shot and he flinched, his hand groping for the butt of his .38 automatic, stuffed into his hip pocket.

He paused at the head of the alley. Across the way, he could see his parked car. The doorman of the Casino was looking tensely away to his right. A scattering of people, enjoying the hot, night air, stood motionless, also looking in the same direction. Then Mish saw two Security guards, guns in hand, come running down the steps of the Casino and go off to the right.

Mish gave up the idea of using his car. He turned left and, not walking too fast, he made his way under the arc lights that floodlit the face of the Casino. During the seconds he had to walk under the blazing lights, he expected to hear shouts or the bang of a gun.

What the hell happened? he wondered, wiping the sweat off his face. Then suddenly he was out of the light and into the shadows.

A familiar voice said, "Keep moving. I'm with you."

Chandler had appeared and fell into step beside him.

"What happened?" Mish asked, not pausing.

"Shut up!" Chandler snapped. His face was white and his eyes glittering. There was an edge of panic in his voice that set Mish's nerves tingling. "Let's get down to the beach! For God's sake, don't run!"

"Who said I was going to run! Goddam it! What happened?"

"Shut up!" Chandler repeated, slightly hurrying his stride.

In a few moments, as the wail of a police siren cut the air, the two men reached the promenade. They plunged down on to the beach.

Not far from them was a party of young people, grouped around a barbecue, its charcoal fire making a splash of red in the moonlight, the smell of grilling steaks savoury in the hot, still air. They were too busy laughing and talking to notice the two men as they slid into the shadows of the languidly swaying palm trees and sank on to the sand.

"What the hell happened?" Mish demanded, ripping off the blouse of his uniform. He felt stifled.

"Trouble . . . it's a murder rap now," Chandler said, trying to steady his voice. "That punk Perry shot a guard!"

Mish had spent too many years of his life mixing with killers to be impressed by violence.

"How about the money?"

Chandler took a long, deep gulping breath. His body was now jerking and shuddering as he remembered how Perry had slaughtered the tough Irish guard.

"We got it . . . Maisky ran out on us . . . he took the money with him."

Mish regarded him, his small eyes narrowing.

"What's the matter with you? What are you so worked up about?"

Chandler swung around and grabbed hold of Mish's shirt front.

"Didn't you hear what I said? That bastard Perry killed . . ."

Mish's heavy, fat hand slapped across Chandler's face, sending him flat on his back. Chandler lay motionless, staring up at the brilliant stars that pinpointed the dark sky. He lay there for some moments, then with a shuddering breath, he sat up.

"Okay, Jess," Mish said quietly. "Relax. So Maisky has the money. Fine . . . I told you he was a bright boy. You don't have to worry about him. Never mind Perry . . . that's just too bad. What happened to Wash?"

Chandler fingered his aching face.

"I don't know."

Mish stared at him, stiffening.

"What do you mean . . . you don't know?"

"There was a guy there . . . an old man . . . he let off a gun. He nearly nailed me. We ran for it. I didn't worry about Wash or Perry . . . they are big enough to look after themselves. I don't know what happened to either of them."

Mish didn't like this, but he guessed he would have done the same thing.

"How much money do you reckon we've got?" Mish asked.

"We haven't got it! Maisky's got it!" Chandler exploded. "The little rat took off as soon as there was trouble!"

Mish stared at him.

"What are you talking about? What the hell did you expect him to do . . . stick around so they could grab the money back?"

Chandler hadn't thought of this possible explanation. He asked more hopefully, "You think that's what happened? I got the idea he was ratting on us."

"Oh, for Pete's sake! Maisky wouldn't do that. I know him. You think for a minute . . . trouble started: he knew you guys could look after yourselves so he took care of the money . . . he beat it. I would have done the same. I'll bet he's right now at the bungalow, waiting for us to join him . . . that's what we arranged, isn't it?"

Chandler began to relax.

"Yeah." He shook his head, trying to convince himself. "When he took off, I really thought . . ." He paused, then shrugged. "We had better get back to the bungalow. It's a hell of a walk."

"How much do you reckon you got?"

"I don't know. We crammed that carton full of money. Exactly how much I have no idea. We had to work fast." Chandler pulled from his hip pockets two thick rolls of bills. "There's quite a lot here . . . all in five-dollar bills."

Mish eyed the money and drew in a deep breath.

"Looks nice, doesn't it?"

Chandler hesitated, then gave him one roll and put the other back in his hip pocket.

"We'd better get moving." He looked uneasily across the beach. There were still too many people in the sea and on the beach for comfort. "These damn uniforms . . ."

"Take 'em off," Mish said and stripped off his khaki shirt. "Turn the pants into shorts and no one will take a second look at us." He found a penknife in his pocket and, taking off his slacks, he began to saw at the legs. In a few moments he was back in the slacks, now turned into shorts.

"Yeah . . . that's an idea," Chandler said, taking off his slacks, and using Mish's penknife, he also completed the same operation.

When they had buried the shirts and the cut-off trousers' legs in the sand, they got to their feet.

"Let's go," Mish said.

They moved out of the shadows and headed towards the sea. They had to pass close to the group around the barbecue. One of the girls, in a bikini and slightly drunk, waved to them. Mish waved back, but kept walking.

The two men, walking easily, not hurrying, headed towards Maisky's bungalow.

Jack Perry shed his I.B.M. blouse and dropped it behind a flowering shrub. The moment the truck had taken off, he had slid away with the swift, silent movements of a jungle cat, not up the path, but through the hedge, across the soft earth, moving away from the Casino. As he slid through the trees and bushes, he unscrewed the silencer on his gun and dropped it into his hip pocket. He knew that within minutes the police would seal off all exits from the Casino. He knew also the old man would sooner or later give the police a description of him. He should have killed him, he thought. He now had to make his own way back to Maisky's bungalow. This was a two-mile walk, and it would be dangerous.

By now he had reached the promenade. He was conscious of looking out of place in his khaki shirt and slacks as a group of young people came towards him, wearing only bikinis and swimming trunks. He kept on, seeing that they looked at him. When he was clear of them, he took off his shirt and tossed it behind a tree. His gun bothered him. It wasn't easy to conceal. Holding it in his hand, down by his side, he kept walking. After some five minutes, he left the promenade and struck off across the sandy beach. Here, it was quiet and less frequented. He paused suddenly as he saw some hundred yards ahead of him a small sports car, parked under a palm tree. By it stood a girl, slipping a sweat shirt over her bikini.

Perry's evil blue eyes darted to right and left. There was no one near the girl. He moved forward.

He arrived by the car as the girl, now seated at the wheel, was slamming the car door shut. She looked up, startled as Perry appeared by her side.

"Hello, Toots," he said with his giggling laugh. "You and me are going for a little drive," and he rested the cold barrel of his gun against her cheek. "Get the photo?"

He couldn't see much of the girl, except her hair was long, wet and dark. The moonlight fell on her breasts, covered by the white sweat shirt, and he told himself she was quite a woman. Perry liked women. Even now, at the age of sixty-two, lust like a misshapen dwarf rode always on his thick shoulders.

The girl caught her breath sharply and Perry dug the gun barrel deeper.

"No fuss, chick," he said. "One little yap out of you and I'll blow your pretty face apart."

He opened the car door and slid into the passenger's seat. He waited a few seconds to allow the girl to recover from her shock, then he lowered the gun.

"Let's go . . . I'll tell you where."

With a shaking hand, the girl thumbed the starter and then engaged gear. She drove the small car off the beach and up on to the road that led away from the promenade.

She knew she was in deadly danger. This fat man, sitting so relaxed by her side, filled her with a nightmare terror. She drove automatically, unable to speak, her heart fluttering, a knotted ball of fear coiled like a spring inside her.

Perry said, "What's a pretty girl like you doing out on the beach alone?"

She said nothing. She could see the glint of the gun in

the shaded dashlight, the barrel pointing at her body, and she shivered.

"You don't have to be this scared," Perry said. His continual giggle increased her fear. It was the most horrible sound she had ever heard. "What's your name, baby?"

Still she couldn't speak. Her tongue felt like a strip of dry leather in her mouth.

Perry put his hot, sweating hand on her naked knee. His touch made her shy away violently. The car swerved, mounted on the grass verge and then bounced back on the road.

Cursing, Perry put his foot across hers and stamped on the brake. The car jerked to a stop and the engine stalled. They were in this narrow road, overhung by trees. There were no villas. It was a road seldom used and leading eventually to the sea. The headlights of the car showed a long tunnel of darkness ahead of them. There was no sound, no movement.

Perry switched off the headlights. The tiny parking lights made a faint splash of yellow on the road. He took the girl by the nape of her neck and gently shook her.

"What's the matter with you, baby . . . scared of me?" he asked and giggled.

The girl's mouth formed into an O. Her sun-tanned face with its small features was grotesque with terror. Suddenly, as if the coil inside her had become released, she began to scream. Perry's thick fingers shifted around her throat and nipped the screams off. Then frantically, wild with panic, she began to struggle, beating his face and chest with her small fists, thrashing with her legs.

Cursing, Perry let his gun slip to the floor of the car so he could use his other hand to control her. She had no chance against his strength. His fingers tightened around her throat, his left hand holding her wrists. He choked her into submission. Then aroused by the contact of her slim, half-naked body, he leaned over her, opened the car door and shoved her out on to the road. She sprawled on the sandy surface, only half conscious as Perry got out of the car and knelt over her.

She was dimly aware that he was ripping off her sweater and her bikini. She became aware of a sharp stone grinding into her spine, but that was nothing to the pain when he thrust into her body, brutally and with animal violence.

Finally, his lust satiated, he heaved himself from her and stirred her with his foot.

"Come on, baby," he said impatiently. "This is for the record. Come on . . . up on your feet," then when she continued to lie at his feet, he reached down, twined his thick fingers in her hair, and hauled her upright. She collapsed against him, moaning, but he shoved her, naked, into the car, his hands sliding over her shivering body.

"Come on . . . come on . . . I've got to get going," he snarled and walked around to the passenger's seat.

Her foot touched the gun. Still half conscious, feeling herself bleeding, not fully understanding what she was doing, she picked up the gun as Perry dropped his heavy body into the passenger's seat. She aimed the gun at him, and sobbing, she pulled the trigger.

Perry saw the flash of the gun, heard the bang and then felt white hot pain grip his bowels. He sat motionless, stupefied, unable to move, his mouth falling open, cold sweat breaking out on his fat face.

He watched the girl roll out of the car, get to her feet and then run naked with lurching strides out of the dim light of the parkers. He smelt the cordite of the exploded shell acrid in his nostrils, then he felt blood seeping into his trousers.

Somehow he managed to shift his wounded body from the passenger's seat into the driving seat. He started the engine, found the right gear and let in the clutch. He headed the car down the tunnel of darkness, knowing he just had to reach Maisky's bungalow before he bled to death.

Maisky edged the Buick into the hide. He was having great difficulty with his breathing and he was now seriously alarmed. The dull pain in his chest was acute. He was feeling on the point of collapse. He had been mad, he told himself, to have tried to shift the carton without unloading it. He had probably strained his heart. He snapped off the headlights.

Well, he would now have to rest. Here, he was safe. He was sure of that. The police would never think of looking for him in this glade. The thing to do was to get up to the cave, taking it slowly, then lie down on a bed of blankets. In an hour or so, he would feel better.

But when he opened the car door and began to get out, a shocking pain struck him in his chest, making him fall back against the seat, his clawlike hands clutching at his chest. For a horrible moment, he thought he was going to die.

He half lay, half sat, waiting, and the pain gradually receded: like a savage animal that had pounced, struck at him, and then drawn back.

He realised he had suffered a heart attack, and his thin lips came off his teeth in a snarl of frustrated fury. After all his planning, all his trouble, the danger and the risks he had taken and just when he was within sight of owning two million dollars . . . this must happen to him!

He remained motionless for more than an hour, trying to breathe gently, terrified to move lest the pain struck him again. He thought of all the money locked in the boot. There was no hope now of getting it up to the cave. It would have to remain in the boot and he would have to hope the hide was good enough to conceal the car should someone pass near by, but it was essential to him, somehow, to get himself up to the cave where the contents of his medical chest might save him.

As he lay waiting for his strength to return, he thought of the young man he had shot. How long would his body remain undiscovered? Had anyone heard the shot? There had been a number of transistor radios blaring on the beach. Their noise might have covered the sound of the shot. The police were certain to connect the shooting with the robbery. The truck was there to tell them. He wondered if the others had got away. The chances were that they had, but if one or more were caught, would they talk? Would they give the police a description of him?

He was now beginning to feel a little better, although very weak. Cautiously, holding on to the side of the car, he drew himself upright. He waited, thinking of the steep climb to the cave with dismay. Well, if it took him the rest of the night, he just had to get up there.

Before starting off over the rough grass, he looked at the boot of the Buick. He again thought of all that money, alive in his mind, but locked out of sight. There was nothing he could do about that . . . anyway, for the moment. Perhaps after a good sleep and a rest, he would be fit enough to move the money up to the cave.

Walking very slowly, his hand pressed against his chest, Maisky made his way cautiously up to the cave.

Mish and Chandler reached Maisky's bungalow around four a.m.

The bungalow stood under a group of palm trees within fifty yards of the sea. It was served by a narrow road that went on to a number of small bungalows and cabins, out of sight and some distance away.

As the two men approached the shabby little building, Chandler caught hold of Mish's shoulder, halting him.

"There's a car . . . look . . . to the left."

In the shadows, Mish could just make out a small car parked to the left of the bungalow. He squinted at it, frowning, then he pulled his gun from his hip pocket.

"That's not Maisky's car . . . it's a sports job."

"Whose then?"

"Let's go and find out," Mish said and began a cautious move forward.

"You don't think . . . the cops?" Chandler hung back.

"Not in a sports job . . . it's a T.R.4," Mish said impatiently.

The two men approached the car, keeping in the shadows. They paused when they were twenty yards or so from it and looked at the bungalow, which was in darkness.

"Maybe he had trouble with the Buick," Chandler said. "It's a bad starter. Maybe he used this one if he couldn't get the Buick to start."

"Yeah . . . that could be it," Mish said, relaxing. "I tell you, he's a real smart cookie. Yeah . . . that must be it," and he walked quickly to the T.R.4 and paused beside it.

The light of the coming dawn was spreading across the sky and the light was sufficient for Mish to see the dark stains on the white leather of the bucket seats. He frowned at them and looked at Chandler who had joined him.

"What's this?"

Mish touched one of the stains with his finger tip, feeling wet stickiness, and then holding his hand up to the growing light, he drew in a sharp broath.

"Judas! It's blood!"

"Maybe he was hit," Chandler said, uneasily. "He could be dead in there."

They moved quickly up the path that led to the front entrance of the bungalow, paused, listened, then Mish, gun in hand, eased open the door and the two men stepped into the stuffy, tiny hall.

"Maisky?" Mish said, raising his voice. "You there?"

"No . . . I am . . ." Perry said from the living-room. There was no giggle in his voice and it sounded far away. "Get in here quick!"

Mish jerked open the door, stared into the gloom, then his hand groped for the light switch, found it and snapped it down.

Perry sat in an armchair. He held a blood-soaked cushion against his belly. There was blood on the floor, his right trouser leg was black with blood. His washed-out blue eyes were slightly out of focus.

"I'm bleeding like a goddam pig," he said huskily. "Do something about it!"

While Chandler stood staring at him, Mish went quickly into the bathroom and opened the cabinet door above the washbasin. His small eyes narrowed when he saw the cabinet was empty. He remembered the previous day when he had cut his hand opening a can of beer, Maisky had taken him into the bathroom and the cabinet had been well stocked with all kinds of first-aid and medical equipment.

He ran into Maisky's bedroom, opened one of the drawers in the chest to find that empty too. Cursing, he snatched off the cover from the bed, ripped a sheet off and came back into the sitting-room.

Mish had dealt with many wounds in his past. He snapped to Chandler to get hot water and to hurry.

Twenty minutes later, Perry was lying on the settee. His fat face was drained white, but his wound had been skilfully bandaged. For the moment, at least, the bleeding had stopped.

While Mish was working on Perry, Chandler had gone through the bungalow.

"The bastard ratted on us!" he said, returning, his face white with rage. "I told you! He's pulled out!"

Perry opened his eyes.

"Get that car out of the way. Dump it somewhere. If the cops spot it . . ." He tried to go on, but faintness overtook him and his eyes closed.

Mish and Chandler looked at each other.

"Yeah . . . you lose it, Jess," Mish said. "If someone spots those bloodstains, we'll have the cops here like a swarm of bees."

"He ratted on us!" Chandler repeated.

"One thing at the time . . . get rid of that car!"

Chandler hesitated, then left the bungalow. Mish watched him through the window get in the car and drive away.

He looked around the room, saw a half bottle of whisky on the table and made a drink.

"Here . . ." he said, bending over Perry, who drank greedily.

"The little bitch . . . she shot me . . ." Perry murmured. He giggled. "She was a good lay . . . she . . ." He drifted off into unconsciousness.

Mish wiped his sweating face. There was a battered radio on one of the bookshelves and he turned it on. Then going into the kitchen he got a pail of hot water and a swab and, returning to the living-room, cleaned up the mess of blood on the floor. He also washed the armchair, although he couldn't entirely efface the bloodstains.

A voice suddenly broke in over the swing music: "We interrupt this programme of dance music coming to you from Paradise City Station XLL with a news flash. The Great Casino robbery. The police have issued the following descriptions of the three men wanted in connection with the robbery . . ." There followed a fairly accurate description of Mish, Chandler and Perry. "These men are dangerous. If seen, please telephone Police Headquarters. Paradise City 7777."

Mish grinned uneasily. Well, the heat was now on. That old man in the glass box wasn't such a dope as he had looked. He snapped off the radio.

He poured himself a shot of whisky, drank it and then went into the kitchen. The refrigerator was empty and so was the store cupboard. Mish rubbed the back of his neck. He was hungry. Worried, he went back and stood looking down at Perry, shaking his head.

Perry had been shot in the stomach. The bullet had cut through a layer of fat and had nicked an intestine. Mish knew the wounded man badly needed hospital treatment, but that was out of the question.

What did he mean about a girl shooting him? Mish wondered.

He poured himself another drink, lit a cigarette, then cursed when he saw he had only two more left in the pack.

He was sitting brooding when Chandler, twenty minutes later, returned.

"Okay?" Mish asked.

"I dumped it." Chandler was jumpy. "Way out on the beach behind a sand dune. Listen, Mish, on the way back, I've been thinking. We better get the hell out of here . . . go back to our hotels and sweat it out. At least we have some money."

Mish grinned.

"Not a chance, boy. It came over the radio half an hour ago. They have our descriptions. You haven't a hope of getting back to your hotel or getting out of the City. We have to stay right here if we are going to survive."

Chandler stared at him, his face tight with frustrated rage.

"Do you think he's coming back?"

Mish shook his head.

"No . . . I guess he's taken us for suckers. Beats me . . . I really thought I could have trusted him. He's pulled out . . . taken everything with him and the dough."

"If ever I run into him again I'll kill him!" Chandler said.

Mish shrugged.

"One of those things, boy, but at least, we are in one piece." He looked at the unconscious Perry. "Not like him."

Chandler looked coldly at the wounded man.

"Who cares?" He dragged open his shirt collar. "If I don't have a cup of coffee, I'll blow my stack."

"Go ahead and blow it. There's not a damn thing left . . . no food . . . nothing except that whisky. You got any cigarettes?"

"Used my last one." Chandler stared at Mish. "We can't live here without food."

"We show ourselves on the street and we're cooked. We have to stay under cover." Mish thought for a moment, then asked, "Have you any friends here?"

"What do you mean?"

"Someone who would bring us supplies without asking questions?"

Chandler then remembered Lolita. Would she do it? Had she heard the radio description of him and if he contacted her would she give him away to the police? He decided he could trust her. She had been in cop trouble herself . . . nothing bad, but the cops were always shoving her around, stopping her entering the better restaurants, leaning their weight on her.

"You might have an idea," he said. "There is a

girl . . . maybe she would do it. Is the phone working?"

"I don't know . . . should be."

Chandler went over to the telephone, lifted the receiver and listened to the reassuring dialling tone. He concentrated for a few seconds, trying to remember the telephone number she had given him. Was it Paradise City 9911 or 1199? He decided it was the latter number. He was very good at memorising his girl-friends' telephone numbers. He dialled the number and waited. There was a long pause, then Lolita said sleepily, "Yes?"

Chandler nodded to Mish, then in his most persuasive manner, charm oozing out of his deep baritone voice, he began to talk.

five

BY MIDDAY, Chief of Police Terrell had an almost complete picture of the Casino robbery.

Reports, telephone calls, Telex communications between Headquarters and the F.B.I. had swiftly built up a picture of the method of the robbery and a description of the men involved. A set of fingerprints had been found on the tool box left in the Casino's control room. Back came a report from Washington with Mish Collins' photograph and record. Another set of fingerprints found on the glass box at the vault's entrance identified Jack Perry, known as a vicious Mafia killer. They had Jess Chandler's description from Sid Regan, but so far had failed to turn up his record.

Terrell pushed aside the heap of reports and reached for the carton of coffee.

"Time off, Joe," he said and poured the coffee into two paper cups. Thankfully, Beigler reached for one of them and lit yet another cigarette. He had been working non-stop since the robbery and he was feeling bushed.

"Well, we are coming along," Terrell said after a thoughtful sip from his paper cup. "We know four of the men . . . one dead, but there's the fifth. It's a funny thing, Joe, but no one seems to have seen him. We have a good description of the other four, but not the fifth man. I'm willing to bet a buck, he is the man who planned the robbery. We do know he was driving the truck, but no one noticed him at the wheel. When trouble started, he took off. What I'm wondering is . . . did he rat on the others or was it agreed that if trouble started, the other men should look after themselves and he should look after the money? Lewis tells me there are two and a half million dollars missing. That's a lot of scratch. He could have been tempted to take off with it, and ditch the others."

Beigler nodded.

"Where does that get us?" he asked, not unreasonably.

"It's a thought." Terrell finished his coffee, hesitated whether to refill his cup, decided not to and picked up another report. "If he has ratted on the others and we catch any of them, they could talk. I want to find No. 5 very badly."

"We haven't caught any of them yet . . ." The telephone bell rang and Beigler grimaced. "Here we go again." He scooped up the receiver. He listened for several moments, his face hardening, then he said, "Okay, Mr. Marcus . . . sure, I understand. I'll be right over. Yeah . . . I know where you are." He scribbled on a pad, then he repeated, "I'll be right over," and hung up. He looked at Terrell who was looking at him. "That was Sam Marcus. He runs a Self-Service store . . ."

"I know him," Terrell said impatiently. "What about him?"

"His daughter, Jackie, was on the beach last night with a party. They were in a hurry to get home, but as Mr. and Mrs. Marcus were away for the night, Jackie stayed on for a last swim. As she was getting into her car . . ." Terrell listened as Beigler talked, then Beigler concluded, "Here's the pay-off. This man was fat, elderly, white-haired. He was wearing khaki trousers and he had a gun. It looks like Jack Perry. After the creep had raped her, she got his gun and plugged him in the belly. She ran off and he took her T.R.4 . . . but he is wounded. Like it, Chief?"

Terrell's face turned grim.

"Where's the girl?"

"Marcus found her when they came home this morning. She was in shock. The doctor's there now. As soon as she could tell the story, Marcus telephoned."

"Okay, Joe, get over there. Make certain the girl isn't romancing. Perry's description has been on the air. One of her boy-friends might have laid her and she is blaming Perry. Check her story out."

Beigler got to his feet and left the office.

Terrell continued to work for over an hour, then Beigler telephoned him.

"It's a straight story, Chief," he said. "It's Perry all right. Here's a description of the T.R.4."

Terrell made rapid notes, told Beigler to come right back, and hung up. He grabbed another telephone and got through to the Control room.

"Alert all doctors and hospitals that a man with a gun-shot wound in the stomach may seek their help," he said. "I want to know pronto if he does. Get it on the air. Here's a description of a car I want traced." He read out Beigler's description of the T.R.4. "Keep hammering away at it. The punk's wounded, and he won't be far from the car."

As he hung up, Fred Hess of the Homicide Squad came in. His fat face was lined with fatigue.

"They've found a young fella shot through the head on the beach, Chief," he said. "Call just come through. Right by his side is a small truck. It matches the description of the robbery truck except it hasn't the I.B.M. signs, but these could have been ditched. I'm going down there now."

"Dead?"

"Sure . . . his brains are all over the beach."

"Okay, Fred, get down there. I want a report as fast as you can make it. Concentrate on the truck. Dr. Lowis alerted?"

"He's on his way now."

Terrell nodded, then, when Hess had left, he pushed his chair away and got stiffly to his feet. He wandered around his small office, thinking.

Once again the telephone bell rang. This time it was Harry Lewis, calling from the Casino.

"Any news, Frank?"

"Plenty . . . I'm busy right now," Terrell said. "I haven't time . . ."

"That's okay. Look, Frank, I've thought of something that might help. I am now certain the gang must have had inside information. The whole job was so slick. They must have known about the fuse boxes . . . the right time to strike . . . where we keep the money . . . the number of guards. And Frank, here is the clincher. We had a blueprint of the electrical circuit in our files and it's missing!"

Terrell became very alert.

"So?"

"I'll swear it's an inside job. One of our girls—Lana Evans—who works in the vault, hasn't reported for two days. Could be she was got at."

"Know where she lives?"

Lewis gave Terrell the address.

"Okay, we'll check. Thanks, Harry," and Terrell hung up. He picked up another telephone. "Lepski in?"

"Just come in, Chief."

"I want him."

Charlie Tanner smiled at Lepski who was grey with fatigue and still wearing his tuxedo. He had been on the job since the robbery broke, and hadn't had a chance to change.

"The big White Chief needs you, Glamour boy," Tanner said.

Lepski cursed. He was about to take a shower and

change before going out again. He ran up to Terrell's office.

"Yes, Chief?"

"What are you doing . . . got up like that?" Terrell asked.

Lepski drew in a long breath. He suppressed all the swear words that crowded his brain.

"Just haven't had time . . ."

Terrell grinned at him.

"Okay, Tom, relax. Get out of that outfit and get over to this address . . . fast." He told Lepski what Lewis had said. "Could be she was bribed to give the gang information. I wouldn't be surprised if she has skipped. Get a description of her, and we'll get it on the air. Hurry it up!"

Twenty minutes later, Lepski, showered and shaved, climbed out of the police car outside Lana Evans's apartment block and rang on the bell.

Mrs. Mavdick came to the door. She looked beyond him at the police car where two uniformed men were getting out, and she stiffened.

"Miss Evans live here?" Lepski asked.

"That's right. What of it?"

"I want to see her."

"She's out." Mrs. Mavdick thumped her floppy bosom and breathed cachou-scented breath into Lepski's face. "Besides, I don't like police here . . . gives my house a bad name."

"Look, sister, relax with the mouth," Lepski said in his cop voice. "You have us here. Where is she?"

The beady, black eyes became interested and cunning.

"Is she in trouble?"

"Could be. Where is she?"

"I don't know. I can't be expected . . ."

Lepski turned and beckoned to one of the police officers.

"We'll go up and see," he said.

"Oh, no, you don't. I don't have cops in my house." Mrs. Mavdick planted herself firmly in the doorway.

Lepski made it his business to know everyone who

passed through the local courts. He had a photographic memory, and he remembered Mrs. Mavdick. He grinned evilly at her.

"Been doing any shoplifting recently, Ma?" he asked. "Let's see . . . it was last August, wasn't it? You got away with a $25 fine. Are you looking for more trouble?"

Mrs. Mavdick gasped, stepped back, then, pausing for a moment to gather her floppy dignity around her, she went into her room and slammed the door.

Lepski and the police officer climbed the stairs until they came to Lana Evans' apartment. The three bottles of milk and the three copies of the *Paradise City Herald* by the door made them exchange glances. Lepski knocked, tried the door, found it locked, then stepped back and drove his shoulder against one of the panels. The door wasn't built to withstand such treatment.

They found Lana Evans lying on the floor. She had been dead now for the past two days.

The black Persian cat was at the window. Seeing Lepski, it jumped down off the window sill and hurried towards the refrigerator.

An hour later, Lepski brought Terry Nichols into the Chief's office. The youth looked white and shocked, and after regarding him steadily for a moment or so, Terrell waved him to a chair.

"I won't keep you long, Terry," he said. "Sit down. Want a cigarette?"

Nicols shook his head.

"Miss Evans was your *fiancée*?"

"Yes."

"Were you planning to get married soon?"

"We hadn't the money to get married," Nicols said bitterly. "We were trying to save five hundred dollars to fit out a walk-up apartment. We didn't reckon we could save that amount under two years." He shrugged. "Well, it doesn't matter now."

Terrell lifted up a newspaper that concealed the money Lepski had found in Lana's drawer.

"This money was found in her room, Terry. Know anything about it?"

Nicols licked his lips, a sudden sick look in his eyes.

"You really mean you found all that money in her room?"

Terrell nodded.

"No . . . I know nothing about it. I don't understand."

Quickly, Terrell explained his suspicions.

"I think she was got at, Terry. She wanted to marry you and she swallowed the bait. This money bought the way into the Casino's vault. She was in the position to give all the necessary information . . . and she got paid."

Nicols didn't say anything. His stricken face showed his feelings.

"Okay, let's assume that happened. We want to find the man who corrupted her . . . he not only corrupted her, but when he got the information he wanted, he murdered her. We want to find this man. Can you help us?"

"No . . . I know nothing about any man. Lana never told me."

"She never mentioned some man who had befriended her?"

"No."

"She never made an excuse not to see you? Some other date?"

"No. I was at night school every night. We met in the morning on the beach. In the afternoon, I was helping out, delivering for a grocery store. I don't know what she did with herself in the afternoons."

Terrell kept at it, asking question after question, but he didn't get any nearer to No. 5 as he was now calling him.

Finally, he took from his desk drawer the jar of *Diana* hand cream that Maisky had given Lana.

"Know anything about this, Terry? Did you give it to her?"

"No . . . what is it?"

"A hand cream . . . costs $20 a jar. Not the sort of thing I imagine, Lana would have bought herself. I was wondering if you had given it to her as a special present?"

"Neither of us would think of paying $20 for a hand cream," Nicols said, and he looked genuinely shocked.

When he had gone, Terrell put the jar into a plastic bag and called in Max Jacoby.

"Take this down to the Lab boys right away. I want everything they can tell me about it."

As Jacoby was leaving, Hess came bustling in.

"It's the truck all right. We picked up the two I.B.M. signs on a side road," he said, coming to rest at Terrell's desk. "The shot boy was Ernie Leadbeater, a student. At least, we now have something on No. 5. We have clear footprints, and the lab boys are working on them. We know he had a car parked at the murder spot. He drove the truck there, transferred the money to the other car, and it's my bet, as he was leaving, Leadbeater surprised him and got shot. We have casts of the car's tyres. They are pretty old, and the off-side one has lost its tread . . . enough to be able to identify it if ever we catch up with the car."

"How about the truck? Any prints?"

"Yeah, but all belonging to the other men. No. 5 wore gloves. The steering wheel is clean."

He took from a plastic bag three $500 bills.

"These were picked up near the truck."

Terrell took them.

"See if you can trace the truck, Fred. Put as many men as you want on to it. It's a top priority."

Hess went off and Terrell sent the bills down to the lab boys.

A couple of hours later, Church, the head of the lab, called Terrell.

"I'm sending you a detailed report, Chief, but while it is being typed, I thought I'd fill you in to save time. First of all that hand cream is loaded with an absorbent compound of arsenic. It is one hundred per cent lethal. No fingerprints on the jar except hers."

"Wait a second," Terrell said, his eyes narrowing. "How could any ordinary person make up a compound like that?"

"The answer to that one is they couldn't. It's the work of a technician: either someone in the pharmacy trade or possibly a medical man."

Terrell made notes.

"I've given you all the dope," Church went on. "There was a lot of arsenic used and whoever made the ointment must have had access to a large amount, which again points to a dispenser. The casts of the footprints give us some interesting information. This man is slightly built, weighs around one hundred and twelve pounds, walks a little pigeon toed, and is not young . . . between fifty and sixty . . . that kind of age. He had an awful struggle to get the carton out of the truck so I could describe him as frail. That any help?"

"Fine . . . anything else?"

"Those $500 bills you sent over. They are all marked with an invisible ink that shows up under infra-red. I talked to Harry Lewis and he tells me he had one thousand of those bills marked as an experiment. They're all missing . . . so if your man starts spending, we could catch up with him."

"This is more like it," Terrell said. "Looks, at last, we are getting a break."

"The boy was shot with a .25 automatic . . . the kind of gun I'd expect No. 5 to carry. He's certainly a careful bird. No fingerprints anywhere. He must have always operated in gloves."

"Get that report over fast," Terrell said, "and thanks."

Jack Perry died without gaining consciousness a little after seven o'clock a.m. Mish, who had been watching him uneasily for the past hour, saw his jaw go slack and he grimaced. He got stiffly to his feet, rubbing his hand over his sweating face. He touched Perry's pulse, then, satisfied that he was dead, he walked down the passage to the back bedroom where Chandler lay stretched on the bed, sleeping. He shook him awake.

Muttering, Chandler opened his eyes, then, seeing Mish, he abruptly sat up.

"He's gone," Mish said. "Come on . . . we've got to bury him pronto."

Chandler swung his legs off the bed. He was wearing shirt and trousers and he groaned softly as he wedged his feet into his shoes. "Where?"

"Right outside. The sand's soft," Mish said. "It's still early. With luck, we'll get away with it, but we have to hurry it up."

Leaving Chandler with his head under the cold-water tap, Mish left the bungalow and entered the garage. There he found a long-handled shovel. Carrying it out of the garage, his feet sinking into the soft sand, he found a spot near a palm tree and began to dig.

When Chandler arrived, the grave was half finished and Mish was panting. Chandler took the shovel and, working fast, completed the job.

"This do?" he asked, looking up at Mish.

"It'll have to. It's getting on," Mish said. "Come on . . . let's get him out."

Twenty minutes later, the two men stood back and surveyed the smooth surface of the sand. Satisfied, Mish broke off several branches of a palm bush and scattered them over the now invisible grave.

Then the two men returned to the bungalow.

"You think she will really come or do you think she was kidding?" Mish asked as he stripped off his sweat-blackened shirt.

"She'll come, but she won't be here until ten," Chandler said. "I'm going back to bed . . . I'm bushed."

"Think she's heard our descriptions on the radio?"

"She could have, but I doubt it," Chandler said. "But don't worry. She and me are like this," and he held up crossed fingers. He went into the bedroom.

Mish took a shower. He longed for a cup of coffee. He lit his last cigarette, put on his shirt and trousers and returned to the sitting-room. It took him some minutes to clean up the room. Finally, he was satisfied that there were now no telltale traces of Perry's brief stay to arouse suspicion. Then he dropped on to the settee and tried to relax.

At half past seven, he turned on the radio to catch the news. It was then he learned of Wash's death and he grimaced. He hesitated whether to tell Chandler, but decided to let him sleep. Once again the descriptions of the three men were broadcast and, snarling, Mish turned off the radio. They were in a hell of a jam, he thought. Where was Maisky? Mish was sure he couldn't have got past the road blocks. The rat! he thought, clenching his big fists. It was safe to bet that Maisky had this planned from the start and had found himself a safe hide-out.

It was nearly half past ten when a shabby Mini-Cooper pulled up outside the bungalow.

Both Chandler and Mish had been waiting at the window, screened by dirty curtains, for its arrival with growing impatience.

As Lolita got out of the car, Mish said, "Is that her?"

"Yes," Chandler said and got to his feet. "You go into the bedroom, Mish. I have to talk to her. This could be tricky."

Mish regarded the girl, who was wearing skin-tight yellow Capri pants and a scarlet halter. Her sun-tanned skin, her shape, her glistening black hair and her lean, alert face made an impact on him. Some bim! he thought, as he moved quickly down the passage and into the bedroom, leaving the door slightly ajar.

Chandler went to the front door and opened it as Lolita started up the path. She paused, looked searchingly at him, then frowned. Chandler wasn't looking at his best. Unshaven, sweaty, his face tight with tension, he presented a picture that slightly frightened the girl.

"Hello, baby," he said. "Gee! Am I glad to see you!"

He came down the path and joined her, putting his big hands on her arms. "Sorry I look such a mess . . . no nothing in this goddam place. Did you bring the stuff I asked for?"

She looked up at him.

"It's all in the car. What's going on, Jess? Is this your place?"

"Let's get the stuff inside, then we can talk," Chandler said. "Look, baby, will you put the car in the garage?"

He walked to the car and took from it two loaded shopping baskets.

"I'll leave it here, Jess. I can't stay long."

"Better get it out of sight, baby," Chandler said, an edge to his voice. "I'll explain in a moment," and he went into the bungalow, carrying the baskets.

She hesitated, then shrugged. She got in the car and drove it into the garage. She got out, closed the garage doors and walked quickly to the entrance to the bungalow. She entered.

"I'm in here, baby," Chandler said, from the kitchen.

She joined him.

He was busy unpacking the baskets.

"Sweetheart, will you make coffee . . . I'll flip my lid if I don't have some coffee." He found a safety razor and brushless cream. "I'll get shaved. Then we can talk."

"All right, Jess," she said and put on the kettle.

When Chandler had shaved, he went into the bedroom and gave Mish the razor and cream.

"I'll call you in five minutes," he said softly, then returned to the kitchen.

Lolita was pouring coffee into a cup.

"That smells good," Chandler said, taking the cup. He spooned in sugar. "No, I'll take it black." He sipped, sighed, sipped again, then picked up a pack of cigarettes she had brought, broke it open and lit a cigarette.

"What's going on, Jess?"

"Cop trouble," Chandler said quietly. "Me and a pal of

mine are in one hell of a jam. Don't ask questions, baby. The less you know the safer for you."

She poured herself a cup of coffee, then, resting her hips against the edge of the table, she asked, "Is it the Casino job?"

Chandler hesitated, then nodded.

"That's it. It turned sour. The guy who planned it ratted on us. Did you pick it up on the radio?"

"Yes. I guessed it was you." She shook her head. "What are you going to do?"

"You guessed it was me . . . and yet you came?" Chandler said, studying her.

"I was born stupid," she said, giving him a half-smile. "I guess I am a little crazy about you, Jess."

He put down his cup of coffee and went to her, putting his arms around her, drawing her close to him.

"You won't regret it," he said, and kissed her.

She clung to him for a long moment, then pushed him gently away.

"What does that mean, Jess? Don't let your coffee get cold."

"There's still a chance we could find this guy who ratted on us," Chandler said. "He has the money. If we find him, then you and I will go off and take a look at the world together."

"Yes?" She smiled at him. "All my life I've been dreaming about looking at the world. Don't let's count on it. You hungry?"

"I know I am," Mish said from the door.

She looked swiftly at him, then at Chandler.

"This is my pal, Mish Collins," Chandler said. "Come in and have some coffee . . . it's good. This is Lolita."

Mish offered a damp hand.

"I always said Jess could pick 'em," he said, shaking hands. "You said something about being hungry?"

"Just the two of you?" Lolita asked, smiling at Mish.

"Just the two of us."

"Ham and eggs?"

"Oh, boy!"

"Give me some room. Suppose you leave me to fix it? I won't be long."

"Sure," Chandler said and moved with Mish, a cup of coffee in his hand, out of the kitchen and into the sitting-room.

"She knows?" Mish asked as soon as they had closed the door.

Chandler nodded.

"There'll be a reward offered," Mish said. "A big one."

"I know."

The two men looked at each other.

"Think you can trust her?" Mish asked.

"We haven't much choice, have we?" Chandler wandered to the window and looked out. "We have to have food if we are going to stay here. She's our only outside link. Maybe they won't be in a hurry to offer a reward."

Mish sat in an easy chair. He began sipping the hot coffee.

"I didn't tell you . . . Wash got shot . . . he's dead."

Chandler didn't look around. He hunched his shoulders.

"It looked pretty good the way that bastard rat laid it out for us like a pretty dream. Well, maybe we will still find him," he said.

"Think so?" Mish lit a cigarette from Chandler's pack. "I wouldn't bet on it. He's a brass boy and cute. I think we have kissed him and the money goodbye."

Chandler shrugged. He continued to stare out of the window for some minutes, then turning, he abruptly left the room and walked into the kitchen.

Lolita was standing over the fry pan, watching six eggs setting in the pan.

"I've been thinking," Chandler said, coming to stand by her side. "I shouldn't have brought you into this. If they catch up with us and find you here, you could go away as an accessory."

"I know I'm stupid," Lolita said, "but not that stupid.

I've thought of that. You don't have to worry about me, Jess. I told you . . . I'm a little crazy about you. You can't stay here without me, can you?"

"That's right."

She smiled at him.

"Well, then . . ."

He leaned forward and kissed the side of her neck.

"I'll make it up to you, baby."

She began serving up the eggs and the ham.

"I'd better move in, hadn't I?" she said, handing him the plates. "If anyone came here, you couldn't go to the door, could you? While you are eating, I'll drive back to my place and pack a bag. There are a few other things we need. Have you any money?"

He put down the plates, took out the roll of $5 bills and gave her ten of them.

"You're sticking your neck out, baby," he said, wondering a little uneasily if he would see her again.

"It's my neck." She patted his arm. "I won't be long," and moving past him, she went down the passage and out through the front door.

Chandler carried the two plates into the sitting-room. Mish was at the window, watching Lolita as she drove away.

"Come and eat," Chandler said.

"She leaving?"

"She's coming back. She's getting her things . . . she's moving in."

"Want to bet on it?" Mish drew up a chair and sat down.

"She's coming back."

The two men ate hungrily, then Mish said suddenly, "I'm not kidding myself, Jess. We're not going to get away with this caper."

Chandler cut into his second egg.

"The odds are long, but we still have a chance."

"I'm not going back to jail." Mish dipped a piece of ham into his egg yolk. "I've had enough of jail."

"Don't worry," Chandler said. "You won't go back to

jail. You'll go to the gas chamber . . . so will I. This is a murder rap."

"Yeah . . . well, they won't take me alive. I don't know about you. I'd rather have a quick bullet than weeks in the Death House."

"Suppose you shut up?" Chandler said. "I want to enjoy this."

Mish suddenly grinned.

"She can cook, can't she? Think she's talking to a cop right now?"

Chandler pushed away his empty plate.

"Want some coffee?"

"I never say no to coffee."

Chandler went into the kitchen. Mish rubbed the back of his neck, reached for the pack of cigarettes, shook a cigarette out and lit it.

He was staring into space, wondering what eventually would become of him, his eyes bleak and lost, when Chandler came back with the coffee.

six

THE SKY was turning a vivid crimson as the sun sank behind the foothills. Tom Whiteside glanced at his wrist-watch. The time was eighteen minutes after eight.

"We'll use the dirt road," he said. "It'll save ten miles. We should be home in another hour."

Sheila Whiteside said nothing. She had been sulking now for the past hour, ever since they had had the row about the gold watch she wanted as her first wedding anniversary present. As Whiteside had pointed out, the watch cost $180 and where was he going to find that kind of money?

He glanced at her, then away. He was feeling depressed. What a vacation! he thought. He had had an idea that he was asking for trouble when he had insisted that they should go camping. Camping, for God's sake! But how else could they have afforded to spend two weeks away from home? They certainly couldn't have afforded a hotel or even a cheap motel. He had borrowed the camping equipment from a friend for free. It was a pretty good outfit with a fair-sized tent, cooking equipment and sleeping bags. But what a fiasco that had turned out to be! Sheila had stuck her toes in and had refused to cook. This was her vacation, she had declared. If they couldn't afford a hotel, then he could do the cooking. He could run the camp. She was going to sunbathe and do nothing.

Tom squirmed at the memory of those past two weeks. He hadn't been able to master the Calor gas cooker. The food was either burnt or under cooked. Sheila had lazed in the sun, wearing the skimpiest bikini, and the constant sight of her near nakedness had tried Tom almost beyond endurance.

He recalled with frustration they hadn't made love during the whole of those fourteen days. Several times he had made advances during the day, but this was something Sheila just wouldn't tolerate. Then at night she got into her sleeping bag, and how the hell was a man to go into action when his wife was in a sleeping bag? Yet he had to endure the sight of her going around looking like an erotic dream, deliberately showing herself off, until there were times when he was fit to climb a tree.

How was it possible, he was continually asking himself, that a girl with such a body, with such beauty, could be so utterly frigid? What a trap! To look at her, you would think . . . as all his friends thought . . . she was hotter than a red-hot stove. She was tall, broad shouldered with large, firm breasts, a narrow waist, solid hips and long, lovely legs. She had natural ash-blonde hair, violet eyes fringed with thick eyelashes, a wide, beautiful mouth, splendid teeth and high cheekbones. There were times, when her eyes were alive and her lips curved into an inviting smile, that she could pass for Marilyn Monroe's sister.

Since he had been so lucky to have married a girl with her looks and her body and that inviting smile, he naturally expected a sexual appetite to go along with the other assets, but here he had been painfully wrong. The sexual act meant less to Sheila than blowing her beautiful nose in a Kleenex.

As Tom coaxed his 1959 Corvette Sting Ray along the Miami highway, aware that there was no pull in the engine and the compression was getting flabbier with every mile he drove, he thought back to the time—fourteen months ago—when he had first met Sheila.

Tom had reached the age of thirty-two without finding success. He was a commission-only salesman working for General Motors branch in Paradise City. Tall, heavily built, dark, with pleasant, rather ordinary features, he had been struggling ever since he had left school to get into the high-income bracket he was sure his talents deserved. The trouble, of course, he was constantly telling himself and his friends, was that he lacked capital. With capital, a guy with his ideas couldn't fail to hit the jackpot, but without capital . . . well what could you do?

But the real trouble with Tom was that he lacked drive. He was a dreamer. He dreamed of riches, but he hadn't the energy or the ability to make money.

Had it not been for his father, Dr. John Whiteside, now dead, Tom would be out of a job. But some years ago, Dr. Whiteside had saved the life of Claude Locking's wife. This was something Locking, who was the manager of General Motors, could not forget. Because he was grateful to the memory of Dr. Whiteside, he tolerated his inefficient son.

Fourteen months ago, Tom had delivered a Cadillac, Fleetwood Brougham to a rich client who lived in Miami, taking the client's Oldsmobile Sedan in part exchange.

Tom had driven the Sedan back to Paradise City, feeling pretty good as he sat at the wheel. This was the kind of car he should own, he told himself, instead of the crummy Sting Ray that was just about falling apart.

The run from Miami was hot and long, and he had decided, since he had made a good commission on the sale of the Brougham, that he would stop off at a motel for the night, have a decent dinner, get a good night's rest and then go on to Paradise City in the morning.

He pulled into the Welcome Motel around nine o'clock, parking the Sedan in one of the bays. After dinner, he went to his cabin, took a shower and went to bed.

He was tired, relaxed and well fed. He looked forward to a good night's rest, but as he turned off the light, a radio in the cabin next door started up, sending strident swing music through the thin partition and bringing him wide awake.

He lay in bed, cursing the noise for some twenty minutes, hoping that the radio would be turned off. A little after eleven o'clock with the noise still tormenting him, he put on the light, struggled into his dressing-gown and banged on the door of the adjacent cabin.

There was a pause, then the door opened and he found himself face to face with the most intriguingly beautiful girl he had ever seen.

Tom often thought of his first meeting with his future wife. She was wearing a light blue wool sweater that emphasised her firm, overdeveloped bust. Her short black skirt seemed to be painted on her. Her long legs were bare and her narrow feet were in cork-soled sandals.

He thought she was wonderful and over-poweringly sexy, and when she smiled, showing her dazzlingly white, movie-star teeth, he was struck speechless.

"I bet you don't like my radio," she said. "Is that right?"

"Well . . ."

"Okay. I'll turn it off. I'm sorry." She looked beyond him at the Oldsmobile under the parking lights. "That your car?"

"Yes," Tom said, the lie coming easily. He put his hand on the door post and looked at her, his eyes moving over that incredible bust.

"Some car."

He grinned.

"Some girl."

They laughed.

"Why don't you come in?" She stood aside. "I'm Sheila Allen."

He moved into the cabin, closing the door. He watched her turn off the radio, his eyes on the solidness of her hips, feeling his blood move faster, thinking she wouldn't need a pillow under her in bed.

"I'm Tom Whiteside. I don't mean to be a crab. I was trying to sleep."

She waved him to an armchair and sat on the bed. Her skirt rode up and he could see her smooth white thighs. He looked away, rubbing his jaw as he sat down.

"You're lucky to be able to sleep," she said. "I can't sleep. I don't know why it is. I never get off before two."

"Some people are like that." He studied her. The more he looked at her the more infatuated with her he became. "I can sleep any time."

She found a pack of cigarettes, shook two out, lit them and gave him one. There was a slight smear of lipstick on the cigarette. It gave him a bang as he put the cigarette between his lips.

"You wouldn't be going to Paradise City tomorrow?" she asked.

"Why, sure. I live there. Are you going there?"

"Yes. There's a bus around nine . . ."

"Come with me."

She smiled, her big eyes opening wide.

"I was hoping you would say that. You work there?"

"That's right . . . General Motors."

"Gee! That must be a pretty good job."

He waved his hand airily.

"It's not so bad. I look after the whole district. Yeah, I can't complain. What are you planning to do in Paradise City?"

"Look for a job. Think I'll find anything?"

"Sure . . . a girl like you. Any ideas?"

"I'm not much good at anything . . . a waitress . . . a hostess . . . something like that."

"Not much good at anything? Who are you kidding?" He laughed. "You won't have to dig deep . . . not with your looks."

"Thanks . . . I hope you are right."

He regarded her, then asked, "Got anywhere to stay?"

"No, but I guess I'll find something."

"I know a place. I'll take you there. It'll be around $18 a week and it's nice."

She shook her head.

"Not for me. I haven't the money. I can't go higher than $10."

"Had it rough?"

"Rough enough."

"You leave it to me. I'll find you a place. I know the City like the back of my hand. Where are you from?"

"Miami."

"What makes you think Paradise City could be better than Miami?"

"Just a change of scenery. I'm a great one for changing the scene."

"Well . . ." He stared at her, then got to his feet. "I'll be leaving at nine tomorrow morning. That suit you?"

"Suits me fine." She stood up, smoothed down her skirt and then came close to him. "I'll pay for the ride if you want me to."

There was that look in her eyes that made him flush.

"I don't want any payment . . . it'll be a pleasure."

"Most men would." She turned her head and looked at the bed. "That kind of payment."

Tom would have given a lot to have taken her up on the offer, but he found he couldn't. This girl suddenly meant much more to him than a quick roll in the hay.

"Not me," he said, his voice unsteady. "Then nine o'clock tomorrow."

She leaned forward and brushed his lips with hers. The feel of her soft lips against his sent his blood hammering.

"I like you . . . you're nice," she said, smiling at him.

He hadn't slept much that night. The following morning, he drove her to Paradise City and found her a tiny room for $8 a day. Away from her, he found he was continually thinking of her. In the past he had got around and had had a number of girls, but none of them affected him the way this girl did. He called on her the following evening. He had borrowed, without permission, the Oldsmobile Sedan, and he was wearing his sharpest suit. They had dinner at an expensive sea food restaurant on the outskirts of the City. It was understandable that Sheila believed she was being courted by a successful, wealthy young business man.

Ever since Sheila had been dumped, at the age of twelve, by her parents on a State highway and left there to fend for herself, she had been in and out of all kinds of trouble, just keeping clear of the Law. She had always looked older than her years. She was now twenty-two. From being a waitress, a dance hostess, a stripper and a receptionist at a two-dollars-a-night hotel, she had finally become one of Miami's many Call girls. This hadn't lasted long. She had helped herself to the contents of a client's wallet and had had to leave Miami in a hurry. She now had fifty dollars in her purse and she wasn't inclined to look for work. She saw Tom Whiteside was infatuated with her, and she decided the fifty dollars would last long enough to keep her until she married him.

They were married when one dollar fifty remained in her purse. It had been a close thing.

Both of them were in for a sharp disappointment. Sheila discovered that Tom lived in a small, shabby bungalow, left him by his father, and that he was neither wealthy nor successful. Tom found she was completely incompetent to run his home. She was lazy; she was frigid and she was continually asking for money.

They had been married now for twelve months. They made the best of a bad job. It suited Sheila to have a roof over her head and regular meals. It suited Tom to have a glamorous-looking wife. At least, if he didn't get any satisfaction from his marriage, he did bask in the envy of his friends, who thought Sheila was sensational.

He turned off the Miami highway on to the dirt road that led through the pine forest down to the Paradise City highway. He switched on his headlights. The sun had gone down behind the foothills. It was now turning dark.

Sheila said abruptly, "About that watch . . . you may not know it, but any decent husband gives his wife a wedding anniversary present. There's nothing else I want so much. I should have something I want."

Tom sighed. He hoped she had put the goddam watch out of her mind.

"I'm sorry, baby. We just can't afford that kind of money. I'll find you a watch, but it's not going to cost $180."

"I want this watch."

"Yeah . . . I know . . . you told me, but we can't afford it."

"I must have been crazy to have married you," she said with an outburst of bitterness. "All those lies about your success. Success? What a joke! You can't afford anything! We don't even get a decent vacation. Camping! God! I should have had my head examined!"

"Would you kindly shut up?" Tom said. "You're no ball of fire yourself. Look at the way you keep house . . . like a pigsty. All you're any good at is watching TV."

"Oh, knock it off!" Her voice was strident and hard. "You bore me. Mr. Successful who can't afford $180. Mr. Successful . . ." She laughed. "Mr. Cheapie, I would say."

The car slowed and Tom pushed down on the accelerator. The car continued to slow, not answering to the extra gas.

"Do you mind?" Sheila said, heavy sarcasm in her voice. "I would like to get home. You may like this dreary scenery, but I don't. Couldn't we go a little faster?"

The engine gave a splutter and died. They were going downhill and Tom quickly shifted the automatic gear stick into neutral. They continued to coast down the road as he cursed under his breath.

"What's the matter now?" Sheila demanded, rounding on him.

"The engine's packed up."

"It only wanted that. What do you expect with a cripple

like this? So what are you going to do?"

As the road began to climb, the car slowed and stopped. Tom stared into the pools of light made by the car's headlights. Then, shrugging, he took a flashlight from the glove compartment, got out of the car and opened the hood. He had had a thorough training in servicing G.M. cars and it took him only a few minutes to find the gas pump had packed up. There was nothing he could do about this. He slammed the hood shut as Sheila got out of the car.

"We're stuck," he said. "The pump's gone. It's a five-mile walk down to the highway. I might be lucky to catch the last bus. You had better stay here."

"Stay here?" Sheila's voice went shrill. "I'm not staying here on my own!"

"Well, okay, then you better come with me."

"I'm not walking five miles!"

Tom regarded her, exasperated.

"So what do we do?"

"You and your lousy car! What a vacation!"

"Will you shut up about our vacation? I'm sick and tired of you complaining."

"So we spend the night here. Get the sleeping bags out."

Tom hesitated, then went to the back of the car. He got the sleeping bags off the rear seat and found the picnic basket. He was hungry, tired and depressed. He locked the car, then threw the beam of his flashlight to right and left. Seeing a narrow path facing him, he went ahead, and found himself in a tree-surrounded glade.

"Sheila! This will do. We can sleep here. Come on. You want something to eat?"

Maisky, lying in his cave, heard Tom's voice. He sat up, his body stiff with apprehension.

Sheila joined Tom in the glade, muttering as she picked her way over the rough ground. Tom had put down the sleeping bags and was opening the picnic basket.

She sat on one of the sleeping bags, took out a cigarette and lit it.

"The end of a perfect vacation," she said. "Oh, boy! Is

this something for my memory book! I've enjoyed every minute of it!"

Tom found some dry slices of ham, a half a loaf of bread that was brick hard and a half a bottle of whisky.

He poured two big drinks. He gave Sheila some of the ham and half the loaf. She promptly threw the food into the bushes.

"I'd rather starve than eat that muck!" she said furiously and drank the whisky at a gulp.

"Okay . . . starve," Tom said. "I've had about all I want from you tonight." Turning his back on her, he began munching the dry ham.

Leaving his bed of blankets, Maisky crawled to the entrance of the cave. He peered through the branches down into the glade. It was too dark to see anything, but he could hear voices although he was too far away to distinguish what was being said.

He lay on the cold, damp floor of the cave, listening. His body trembled with weakness. Who were these people? What were they doing down there? How long would they stay?

Tom finished his meal, then taking off his windcheater and his shoes, he got into his sleeping bag. Sheila was already in hers.

"Will you try not to snore?" she said. "It only wants you to snore to make this really perfect."

"Just go to hell!" Tom said bitterly, then trying to make himself comfortable, he closed his eyes.

Sergeant Patrick O'Connor, known in the police force as Gutsey O'Connor, was sixty-one years of age. He had been in the Paradise City police now for forty odd years. Six foot three, with an enormous belly that had earned him his nickname, a brick-red face and thinning, sandy hair, he was one of the less-liked sergeants attached to the force.

In another year, he planned to retire. He hadn't done so badly during his service career. He had made a nice slice of money putting the bite on the prostitutes, the pimps, the pushers and the queers who lived in his district. For a $10 bill, he was always ready to look the other way, and although his graft was small, over a period of forty years it had totalled up to a respectable sum.

When Beigler told him to take Patrolmen Mike Collon and Sam Wand and search five hundred bungalows in the hope of finding the missing Casino robbers, O'Connor stared at Beigler as if he couldn't believe his ears, and when Beigler told him to go to the Armoury where he would be issued with tear-gas grenades and automatic weapons, Gutsey O'Connor's red face turned a purplish white.

He had heard all about the Casino robbers. They were desperate, dangerous men—one of them was a Mafia killer!

O'Connor plodded down to the Armoury thinking that this was just his luck. In another year, he would be free of this kind of caper. He would own his own bungalow, his own car and he planned to grow roses. Now he might very easily get himself killed on this goddam assignment.

He found Mike Collon and Sam Wand waiting for him in the Armoury. Both these patrolmen were young and keen. Collon was big, dark and tough looking with a growing reputation for being smart, and with a number of arrests in his book. Wand was shorter, fair, with steel-grey eyes. He too was keen and ambitious. The kind of punks, O'Connor thought sourly, he would get landed with.

"Okay, fellas," he said, "get your weapons and let's go."

He drew an automatic rifle and ammunition from the Sergeant Armourer who grinned unfeelingly at him.

"Watch that big belly of yours, Gutsey," he said. "You don't want anyone to make a hole in it. I reckon there'd be enough gas out of that to light the City for a week."

"Shut your trap!" O'Connor snarled. "All very well for you . . . you just hand out a gun. I've got to use it!"

He stamped out of the Armoury. Collon and Wand exchanged winks. They followed him to the waiting police car and they all piled in. Wand took the wheel.

"North Shore," O'Connor said, "and snap it up."

The time was a little after six o'clock when they reached the first row of bungalows that skirted the beach near the Casino.

The three officers got out of the car.

"Okay, fellas, start working," O'Connor said. "You know what to do. Find out who owns the place. If they've been there some time, skip the search. If they are renting the place, go over it. I'll be right here, covering you."

Wand stared at him.

"Doing what, Sarg?" he asked.

"You deaf? I'm here to cover you," O'Connor barked. "Get moving!"

The two patrolmen looked at each other in disgust, then set off towards the bungalows. They were both aware of the danger of their assignment, but neither of them hesitated. They never had had any use for Gutsey, and this act of blatant cowardice set their seal of contempt on him.

"Good luck, Mike," Wand said as he pushed open the wooden gate, leading to the first bungalow. "Watch it."

"You, too," Collon said, and moved farther down the lane to the adjacent bungalow.

The search progressed fairly swiftly and unsuccessfully. None of the people renting the bungalows objected to letting the police officers in. They had all heard about the Casino robbery, and were thrilled to be on the fringe of such a daring steal.

Around eight o'clock, the two patrolmen had covered forty of the bungalows, and it was now growing dark. Gutsey O'Connor was sitting in the police car, resting his feet and dozing. He was no longer taking any interest in the search, being convinced it was now just routine and the wanted men weren't hiding in his district.

But Wand and Collon didn't relax. They knew that any moment they might turn up these three men and then there would be a battle. Young and as tough as they were, the strain was beginning to tell.

The final bungalow in the long row yielded nothing and they returned to the police car.

"How long do we keep this shindig up?" Wand demanded as O'Connor jerked awake.

"We'd better drive to the South end now," O'Connor said, trying to sound alert. "The Chief didn't say anything about knocking off."

"Sure you wouldn't like to help out, Sarg?" Wand asked sarcastically. "One more man on the job, and we'd get done that much quicker."

"I give the orders around here," O'Connor snapped. "Get in and let's go."

They drove farther down the beach road, past a big clump of palm trees until they came within sight of another long row of bungalows.

Without knowing it, they were now within five hundred yards of Maisky's bungalow. The two patrolmen, their automatic rifles carried at the alert, walked along the sandy road, split up and began rapping on doors again.

At this moment, Mish Collins pushed aside his plate and released a soft belch. That, he told himself, was one of the best meals he had eaten for a long time. Looking across at Lolita who had prepared the meal, there was genuine admiration in his eyes.

"That was swell," he said. Then to Chandler, "Boy! You certainly can pick them!"

Chandler laid down his knife and fork and grinned.

"She's something very special." He patted Lolita's hand. "That was terrific, baby . . . and I mean terrific."

"You men . . . if a woman can cook, you're just mush." Lolita got to her feet. "Sit still. I'll take care of the dishes," and rapidly clearing the table, she carried the dishes into the kitchen.

"This is about our one lucky break," Mish said, lighting a cigarette. He tossed the pack to Chandler. "I really thought she was going to walk out on us."

Chandler got to his feet and moved over to the open

window. It was growing dark now. He could see the moon coming up behind the palm trees, making the sea glitter. He drew the curtains and turned on the light.

"I told you. She and I have an understanding."

"Do you think we are safe here, Jess?"

Chandler sat in an easy chair. He let smoke drift down his nostrils.

"Could be. I don't know. We should work out something, Mish. If the cops did come here, there's a good hide in the roof. If something started, we could leave Lolita to handle it and you and me get up in the roof."

"Think her nerve would hold?"

"Sure."

Mish got to his feet.

"I'm going to grab me some air."

"Watch it."

Mish grinned.

"Relax, Jess. I know what I'm doing."

When he had left the bungalow, Chandler walked into the kitchen where Lolita was finishing the washing up.

"Anything I can do?" he asked.

"It's done." She took off her apron and came over to him. She leaned hard against him as he put his arms around her. "Where's Mish?"

"He's taking the air." Chandler's hands slid down her back and cupped her buttocks. "Let's go to bed, baby." He pulled her close to him.

"I was only waiting for you to say that."

They kissed, then, his arm around her, he led her out of the kitchen, down the passage and into the main bedroom. As he was about to close the door, he heard Mish come in. Mish's movements were hurried. Chandler stiffened. He raised his hand to Lolita, and then stepped into the passage.

"There's a police car down the road," Mish said tensely. "They are checking all the bungalows. They'll be here in half an hour . . . automatic weapons."

Lolita came to the door, zipping up her dress.

"What is it?"

"The cops . . . they're checking the bungalows," Chandler said, trying to keep his voice steady.

Mish pointed to the trap door in the ceiling.

"We'll get up there."

"Put the radio on," Chandler said to Lolita. "When they come . . ."

She was surprisingly calm: a lot calmer than Mish and Chandler.

"I know. You don't have to tell me. I'll handle it, Jess. Just get up there and leave it to me."

"This could turn into a jam, baby," Chandler said. He had a sudden spasm of conscience. He had no right to ask her to do this for him. "Maybe you had better go. You still have time . . ."

"Get up there and be quiet. I'll handle it."

He pulled her against him.

"You won't regret this. When we do get out of this mess, you and I . . ."

She smiled up at him.

"I know, Jess."

Mish brought a step ladder from the kitchen. He opened the trap door and hauled himself into the hot space between the roof and the ceiling.

Chandler kissed Lolita, then he climbed up into the roof. Looking down at her, he said, "You are going to handle this beautifully, and I love you."

"I love you too," she said and carried the step ladder back into the kitchen.

Chandler let down the trap door, then he took his gun from his hip pocket and snicked back the safety catch.

"Remember, Jess," Mish said out of the darkness. "It's us or them. I'm not going back to jail."

It was after ten o'clock when Wand and Collon walked around the thick, high clump of tropical shrubs and palm trees and came suddenly on Maisky's bungalow.

Both men came to an abrupt standstill, their sweating hands gripping their automatic rifles, turning their knuckles white.

They stared at the isolated bungalow, seeing a light coming through the curtains of one of the windows.

"If they are anywhere," Collon said, "this could be it."

Both men were now so jumpy after their four hours of continual checking that they both hesitated. Every door they had knocked on, they had expected to be received by a blast of gunfire. They were now in a demoralised state.

"Look, Mike," Wand said, "I've had enough of this. Let's get Gutsey to handle this one."

"Yeah."

They turned and moved around the palm trees out on to the beach, they signalled to O'Connor who was sitting in the police car, the glowing end of his cigarette showing through the windscreen.

They had to signal three times before O'Connor, cursing under his breath, started the car and drove up to them.

"What's the matter?" he demanded, glaring at them through the open window of the car.

"There's a lone bungalow just around the trees," Wand said. "We think you should handle it, Sarg."

"What the hell do you mean?" O'Connor exploded. "I'm covering you, ain't I? You go ahead. Hear me? That's an order."

"They could be there," Wand said. "You're coming with us, Sarg, or I will turn in a report to the Chief."

O'Connor glared at him. "About what?"

"That you sat in the car on your fat fanny and let us handle the search. And I'll do it, Gutsey, even if I get thrown off the force!"

"You call me that again and I'll knock your goddam teeth out!"

"Fine, Gutsey . . . try and do it," Wand said quickly.

O'Connor wiped the sweat off his face. He got out of the car. He was four inches taller than Wand and three times as heavy. He doubled his thick fingers into an enormous fist.

Collon said softly, "You hit him, Sarg, and I'll hit you."

O'Connor regarded Collon's big frame; he was built like a heavyweight champion, and he was young and very tough.

"You two are in real trouble," O'Connor snarled. "Okay, we'll go back to headquarters. I'm putting you both on a charge."

"Fine. The Chief will love it," Wand said. "We arrive at the one place these hoods could be hiding, and you chicken out and bring us back on a charge. Okay, Sarg, if that's the way you want it, let's go back to headquarters. I bet you'll kiss your pension goodbye."

O'Connor glared at him, hesitated, then cursed.

"You wait until I get you two back to headquarters."

"Do you check this bungalow or do we go back?" Wand asked.

Again O'Connor hesitated, but he knew he was trapped. Muttering under his breath, he began walking slowly across the sand until he came within sight of the isolated bungalow. He stopped abruptly. He now saw what these two jerks meant. This was just the place where the wanted men might be. He stared at the light coming through one of the curtained windows, and sweat ran down his fat face.

"You going ahead, Sarg?" Wand asked politely, "or are we staying here the rest of the night?"

O'Connor turned.

"You two guys go ahead. I'll cover you," he said.

"Not us, Sarg. *You* go ahead. *We'll* cover *you*," Wand said.

"Think they're in there?" O'Connor said, hesitating.

"You find out, Sarg."

Slowly, O'Connor began to walk forward. His fat legs were shaky. The other two followed him. He reached the wooden gate that guarded the short path to the bungalow. Here, he paused.

"I'll go around the back," Collon said and moved off into the darkness.

When he had gone, O'Connor said, "Look, Sam, I'm an old man. You go ahead. I swear I'll cover you."

"Not me, Sarg. I'm a young man. I've got a lot longer to live than you have. They could give you a medal."

Livid, O'Connor turned on him.

"Listen, you jerk, I'll make your life a misery! You're refusing to obey an order. You hear me! Go . . . knock on that door!"

"I'd rather lead a life of misery than have a dead one," Wand said. "You knock on the door. We've already knocked on a hundred doors. You try it for size, Sarge."

Then the door opened and a girl came out into the moonlight. The light from the hall lit up her silhouette. She was wearing a short, white dress, and the light showed her legs up to her crotch through the dress.

O'Connor drew in a long breath of relief. Scarcely believing his luck, he walked up the path as the girl came towards him.

"Is there something wrong?" she asked. "It's the police, isn't it?"

O'Connor reached her and stared down at her. Some bim! he thought. There I was, scared crap silly, and look what comes out of the goddam place!

Wand was close on his heels. The two policemen regarded the girl as she looked from one to the other.

"You live here?" O'Connor asked, pushing his peaked cap to the back of his head and wiping the sweat off his forehead with a grubby handkerchief.

"Of course." She gave him a dazzling smile.

"Been here long?"

"A couple of weeks . . . I rent the place. What is it, Sarg?"

"Aw, forget it," O'Connor said and grinned. "We're just checking. Didn't mean to scare you, Miss."

"Do you mind if we look inside?" Wand said quietly. He was staring at the girl, wondering where he had seen her before. He had seen her. He was sure of that, but where? "You are alone?"

"Yes, I'm alone," Lolita said. "Go ahead . . . take a look. What are you looking for?"

As Wand started forward, O'Connor grabbed his arm.

"Stop leaning your weight on everything," he growled. "We don't have to worry the little lady. Come on, we still have work to do."

Hearing voices, Collon came around from the back of the bungalow.

"Come on . . . come on . . ." O'Connor said impatiently. He was so relieved that he had escaped trouble, he couldn't get away fast enough. "Leave her be," and giving the girl a salute, he started off down the path.

Wand was still staring at Lolita. Then he suddenly remembered where he had seen her. She had been singing and playing a guitar in a restaurant near the harbour. His quick mind told him a girl like her couldn't afford to pay the rent of a bungalow in this district.

She was smiling at him.

"Do you want to come in?"

"Yeah . . . I'm coming in. You lead the way."

She turned and moved into the bungalow, swaying her hips.

"Some chick," Collon said admiringly.

"Watch it," Wand said out of the corner of his mouth. "This could be it." He snapped off the safety catch of his rifle. Collon stared at him and seeing his white, set face, he felt a prickle of excitement run up his spine.

O'Connor had reached the gate. He turned and looked back up the path.

"Come on, you jerks!" he shouted. "What are you doing?"

Wand moved into the bungalow. Collon, aware now that Wand was more than suspicious, followed him closely, his thumb snapping back the safety catch on his rifle.

"Stay right here," Wand said softly, "and cover me. Watch it!"

He walked into the living-room. The first thing he noticed was an ashtray on the table loaded with cigarette butts: only a few of them had lipstick smears.

Lolita turned off the radio. She seemed completely at ease and her smile was inviting.

"Go ahead . . . look around. Can I get you boys a drink?"

"No thanks," Wand said. He moved past her into the kitchen. He saw three plates in the drying rack, three knives and forks lying on the draining board, and his skin prickled. He opened the refrigerator and looked at the vast stock of food. He knew then that somewhere in this bungalow were the wanted men. Walking as if on eggshells, his rifle pushed forward, his finger on the trigger, he opened the three doors, one after the other, that led into the bedrooms. In the main bedroom, hanging over the back of a chair, he saw a man's red and blue tie.

He came out into the passage, looked to right and left, then up at the trap door in the ceiling.

Lolita came to the sitting-room door.

"All right?" she asked. The strain was beginning to tell, but she still managed an inviting, convincing smile.

Wand moved forward, riding her back into the sitting-room.

"Okay, sister," he said, speaking low, "they're up in the loft, aren't they?"

Her eyes widened for a brief moment, then she forced a smile, but this time it was a lot less convincing.

"They? I don't understand. What do you mean?"

"I know you," Wand said. "You couldn't afford to live in this place. You better open up or you'll be in real trouble. They are up there, aren't they?"

Lolita's lips were now pale under her lipstick, but she didn't give up.

"They? I told you . . . I'm alone here. What is all this about?"

Wand walked to the door.

"Get Gutsey," he said to Collon.

Collon went to the front door and waved to O'Connor

who was standing by the gate, waiting impatiently. Uneasily, the fat sergeant came up the path.

"What the hell is it now?"

"Take her," Wand said. "They're up in the loft."

O'Connor gaped at him, then he caught hold of Lolita's arm. He jerked her into the passage as Mish, listening to all this, gently raised the trap door, aimed his gun and squeezed the trigger.

The gun exploded with a bang that rattled the windows. A red stain appeared on O'Connor's tunic. He went down on his knees, like a stricken ox, his hands clasping his enormous belly.

Lolita screamed and threw herself back into the sitting-room as Collon, jerking up his rifle, ripped in shot after shot through the ceiling.

Mish, hit in the face and through the body, somehow lifted his gun and again squeezed the trigger. Shot through the shoulder, Collon dropped his rifle, falling face down on the floor. Mish tried to regain his balance, then toppled through the trap door, his dying fingers squeezing the trigger of his gun which exploded bullets through the narrow passage. He thudded down on Collon as Wand shot him again through the head.

Wand hurriedly backed into the sitting-room, crouching down on one knee. There were two more of them up there, he thought, not knowing that Jack Perry was already dead.

Carefully sighting his rifle at the already holed ceiling, he fired five quick shots into the ceiling.

"Okay, you two," he bawled. "Come on down with your hands in the air!"

Lolita, standing against the wall, looked wildly around the room. Her eyes alighted on a heavy glass ashtray. Without hesitating, she reached for it, took three silent steps up to Wand who was staring through the doorway at the open trap and crashed the ashtray down on his head.

He dropped the rifle, gave a groan and fell forward.

Her heart hammering, she jumped over his body and ran to the trap door.

"Jess! Quick! Come down!" she screamed. "We can get away! Come down quick!"

There was a pause, then a scuffling noise and Chandler appeared in the open trap. His face was white and his eyes half closed.

"Beat it, baby," he said hoarsely. "There's nothing more you can do for me now . . . and thanks for everything."

Blood ran out of his mouth and dripped on to the worn mat in the hall.

Lolita screamed.

"Jess!"

"Beat it," Chandler gasped, then his eyes rolled back and he sagged forward, his arms hanging close to her face.

She caught hold of his hand, then shuddered and released it. She ran into the bedroom, snatched up her suitcase, threw it on the bed and crammed her things into it. Tears ran down her face and every now and then she caught her breath in a rasping sob.

Carrying the suitcase, she went out into the hall, looked again at Chandler, then, jumping over O'Connor's great bulk, she ran out into the darkness of the garage. She threw her suitcase into the back of the Mini, got in and started the engine.

She drove fast towards the Miami highway.

seven

FOR THE past three hours the Homicide Squad, under Hess, and the fingerprint experts, under Jeff White, had swarmed over Maisky's bungalow.

Chief of Police Terrell, back at headquarters, was waiting impatiently for their reports.

When Sam Wand had recovered consciousness, he had staggered to the police car and triggered off the alarm. Patrolmen at the Miami-Paradise road block had arrested Lolita and had taken her to headquarters. She was now in a cell, waiting to be questioned.

Around midnight, Hess walked into Terrell's office, his fat face shiny with sweat, his eyes dark ringed.

"Well, Fred? What's the news?" Terrell asked as he poured coffee into two paper cups and gave Hess one. The fat detective slumped down on a chair.

"Looks like there's only one left," he said, paused to gulp some coffee, then went on, "No. 5. But there's no sign of the money. O'Connor's dead. Collon has a smashed shoulder, but he'll survive. Here's as far as we've got: the bungalow was rented by Franklin Ludovick on May 2nd last year. He's been living there up to now. He must be our No. 5. The bungalow hasn't been properly cleaned for some time and Jeff has a whale of a lot of prints. He has wired them to Washington. We expect to hear any time now. I've talked to the Agent who rented the bungalow. His description of Ludovick matches the description given us by the Lab boys: sixty-five, small, frail, sandy hair, beaky nose and grey eyes. He owns an old Buick, but the Agent can't remember its colour nor its licence number. He has pulled out. Nothing belonging to him remains in the bungalow. Looks now as if he did rat on the others. Where he is is problematic. We do know he hasn't passed the road blocks."

"All right, Fred. It's a good start," Terrell said. "Nothing yet on the truck?"

"Not so far . . . oh, yes, we've found the T.R.4. It was hidden in the sand dunes, about a mile from the bungalow."

"No sign yet of Perry?"

"It's my bet he's dead. The car is soaked in blood. No man could bleed like that and survive. They've probably buried him some place."

"Well, we are making progress." Terrell finished his coffee. "Now, we have to find No. 5."

Jacoby came in.

"Excuse me, Chief, a signal from Washington just came in."

Terrell read the signal, then looked at Hess.

"Here's our man: Serge Maisky. He spent ten years at Roxburgh jail as a dispenser. He retired April last. They're sending a photo." He laid the signal on the desk. "He's here somewhere, so we take the City to pieces. Where he is, the money will be. Get it organised, Fred. Put on every available man. He shouldn't be all that difficult to turn up."

Hess got wearily to his feet.

"Could be famous last words, Chief. But I'll get it organised," and he left the office.

Terrell reached for the telephone. He told the police matron to have Lolita brought to his office, but he didn't get anywhere with her. She sat, stunned, white faced and silent, not answering his questions, but rocking herself to and fro in her misery. Jess Chandler had been the only man she had ever loved. His death had left her no hope in life. Finally, shrugging, Terrell sent her back to her cell.

Tom Whiteside opened his eyes and blinked up at the sky that showed blue through the canopy of trees. He looked at his wristwatch. The time was twenty after seven. He looked over at Sheila. She was asleep. For a girl who claimed she could never sleep, he thought sourly, she didn't do so badly.

He crawled out of his sleeping bag and shaved with his cordless razor, then, feeling a little more alive, he went down to the car. He got from the boot the hated gas cooker, and after a fierce struggle, got one of the burners to light. He brewed up coffee while he smoked a cigarette.

Then, carrying two steaming cups of coffee back into the glade, he stirred Sheila with his foot.

"Come on . . . come on . . . wake up," he said irritably. "Here's some coffee."

She moved, moaned, then opened her eyes. She looked sleepily up at him.

"Oh . . . you . . ."

"Yes . . . me." He dumped the cup of coffee by her side and went over to sit on his sleeping bag.

He watched her struggle out of her sleeping bag. She was wearing only bra and sky-blue panties. The sight of her as she stood up and stretched set his blood on fire. But he knew he was working himself up for nothing, and he looked away.

She went behind a bush to relieve herself, then came back, snapping the elastic of her panties.

"This I love," she said bitterly. "Crouching behind a bush! What a way to live!"

"Oh, for Pete's sake, shut up!" Tom snarled. "Can't you ever stop complaining?"

She squatted on her sleeping bag and sipped the coffee. After the first sip, she shuddered and threw the rest of the coffee into the shrubs.

"What did you put into it . . . earth?"

"What's the matter with it?" Tom demanded, glaring. He had to admit the coffee tasted like hell. Probably he hadn't waited for the water to boil, but he had made it . . . at least he had done that.

"The matter with it? Don't make me laugh!" She reached for her slacks. "What do we do now? I want to get home."

"Do you imagine you're the only one?" Tom forced himself to finish his coffee although it made him feel slightly sick. "We'll have to walk or do you want to wait here?"

"Wait here? *Alone?* I'm not staying here on my own!"

"Well, okay, then you'll have to walk."

"If you imagine I'm going to walk five miles you need your head examined!"

He drew in an exasperated breath.

"Make up your stupid mind! You either stay or you walk! I'm going right now."

She hesitated. At this moment the rising sun reflected on something close by that glittered. She looked at the glitter, her face puzzled, then she walked over to a high mass of dead branches and peered into the undergrowth.

"Tom! Here's a car!"

"What are you yapping about now?" Tom said impatiently. He was putting on his windcheater.

"Look . . . a car!"

Maisky was lying at the mouth of the cave. He could see them now. His shaking hand gripped his .25 automatic. There was a dull, warning pain in his chest. Slowly, carefully, he lifted the gun.

Tom joined Sheila. Pulling aside some of the dead branches, he discovered Maisky's Buick.

"What's this doing here?" he said blankly.

Sheila dragged more dead branches away. They both stared at the car, then she said, "See if it will start."

"We can't do that. Someone's hunting or something," Tom said uneasily.

"See if it will start!" Sheila screamed at him.

Tom groped in his hip pocket and brought out a set of keys. As a G.M. agent, he always carried a master key for all of their cars. He unlocked the car door, slid under the driving wheel, sank the key into the ignition lock, turned it and put his foot down on the gas pedal. The engine fired.

"Well . . . talk about luck!" Sheila said. "Come on. We'll borrow this and get home. Then you can get a new pump, come back here and fix our ruin."

"We can't do that! We could be arrested for stealing!"

Sheila threw her arms up in exasperation.

"What a jerk you are! Okay, so the guy has to wait a couple of hours. So what? You can explain. You're not stealing the car . . . you're borrowing it."

Tom hesitated, but he saw the sense in this. He got out of the Buick and walked down the path, out of the glade, to where his car was parked. He found in the glove compartment a pad of paper and a ball pen. He wrote:

I have broken down so I have had to borrow your car. I'll be returning in two hours. Excuse me.

Tom Whiteside, 1123, Delpont Avenue, Paradise City.

That should keep him right with the Law, he thought as he fixed the note under his windshield. He hurried back to where Sheila was completing her toilet.

"All right," he said. "Let's go."

She regarded him with that exasperated look of contempt that had so often made him squirm.

"Oh, boy! How bright can you be! Are you going to leave all the camping equipment in the car? Suppose some bum comes along and steals it? Are you going to pay for it, Mr. Cheapie?"

Tom hadn't thought of this and it irritated him.

"Well, okay, okay." He got into the Buick and started the engine.

Maisky tried to aim his gun at him, but in his weak, shaking hand, the gun barrel danced as if it were alive. He cursed as he lowered the gun. With murderous rage and sick frustration, he watched Tom back the Buick, turn it and then drive out of the glade.

Reaching his car, Tom pulled up. Both he and Sheila transferred all their clothes and the camping equipment on to the back seat of the Buick. They were then left with the gas cooker which wouldn't fit into the back of the car.

"Put it in the boot," Sheila said impatiently. She got in the passenger's seat of the Buick and lit a cigarette.

Tom unlocked the boot and opened it. In the boot was a big cardboard carton with the initials I.B.M. painted in black letters on its side. He wondered vaguely what it contained, but as Sheila called to him to hurry up, for God's sake, he put the cooker against the carton and slammed down the lid.

He got in the car and drove down the five-mile-long dirt road until they reached the Paradise City highway.

Sheila was relaxed now, her arm on the window frame of the car. This was the first time in months that she had been in a car that didn't rattle and showed signs of power.

"Why don't you get a better car?" she asked suddenly. "You work for these jerks. Why can't they give you something better than our stinking ruin?"

"Just rest your mouth," Tom said. "If I have anything more from you, I'll go screwy."

"Screwy? Who said you aren't already screwy?"

"Oh, will you shut up!" Tom leaned forward and snapped on the radio. Anything to keep her quiet.

A voice was saying: ". . . the Casino robbery the night before last. Four of the wanted men are now accounted for, but the fifth, believed to be the ringleader, is still at large. The police are anxious to question Serg Maisky, alias Franklin Ludovick, who they think may help them with their inquiries. The description of the wanted man is as follows: age sixty-five, slimly built, height five foot seven inches, thin, sandy-coloured hair, grey eyes. He is thought to be driving a Buick coupe. The police believe he is in possession of a large cardboard carton with the initials I.B.M. painted on its sides. This carton may contain the two and a half million dollars taken from the Casino. Anyone seeing this man is asked to notify the police immediately. Paradise City 7777."

The Buick swerved and a driver, overtaking, blasted his horn and cursed Tom as he stormed past.

"What are you doing?" Sheila demanded. "You could have had a smash," then seeing his white face, she asked sharply, "What's the matter?"

"Shut up!" Tom snapped, trying to control himself. He slowed the car, feeling cold sweat on his face. Had he heard aright? He thought of the big carton in the boot. He saw again the initials I.B.M. painted on the box. Two and a half million dollars!

"You look as if you've swallowed a bee," Sheila said, now worried. "What is it?"

He drew in a long, slow breath.

"Turn the radio off!"

She shrugged impatiently and snapped off the radio.

"What's biting you?"

"I think this car belongs to the Casino robbers," Tom said, his voice strangled. "The money is in the boot!"

Sheila stiffened, staring at him.

"Have you gone crazy?"

"There's a carton in the boot with I.B.M. painted on it!"

Her eyes grew round.

"This could explain why the car was hidden," Tom went on. "What the hell are we going to do?"

"Are you sure about the carton?"

"Of course, I'm sure . . . do you think I'm blind?"

A feverish excitement took hold of Sheila. She remembered what the announcer had said: *This carton may contain the two and a half million dollars taken from the Casino.*

"We'll go straight home and make sure," she said.

"We'd better go to police headquarters."

"We are going home!" Her voice now was hard and shrill. "If the money is really in the boot, we're not handing it over to the police! There'll be a reward . . ."

Tom began to protest, then he saw the traffic was slowing down.

"What's going on?" he said, braking and staring at the long line of cars coming to a halt.

Sheila leaned out of the window.

"There's a road block ahead. The in-going traffic is being waved through. They are only checking the out-going traffic."

Tom drew in a long, unsteady breath.

"We'd better tell them."

"Oh, quiet down! We are going home and we are going to make certain first the money is there!"

Tom was now approaching the road block. He saw Patrol Officer Fred O'Toole waving the in-going cars through. He was friendly with O'Toole. They often played pool together in a down-town bar.

O'Toole grinned at him as he waved him through. "Got a new car, huh?" he called. "Had a good vacation?"

His white face set in a grin, Tom nodded and waved a sweating hand.

"We should have stopped and told him," he said as they continued on down the highway.

"Haven't you any guts?" Sheila said impatiently. "They are certain to offer a big reward. This is our chance, at last, to make some real money!"

"Maybe the money isn't there," Tom said, but he now began thinking of what the radio announcer had said. *Two and a half million dollars!* It turned his mouth dry just to think of such a sum.

"The carton's there, isn't it?"

"Yes."

"Well, then. Let's get home, and don't drive too fast! We don't want some traffic cop . . ."

"Okay, okay, stop shouting at me! I know what I'm doing!"

"I wish you did. You look like a pregnant duck."

"Oh, shut up!"

They drove the rest of the way in silence. As they reached Delpont Avenue, Tom slowed. They drove down the long, shabby avenue, lined either side with small cabins and bungalows. The time was now half past nine. It was a good time to arrive. The owners of the cabins and bungalows had already left for work, and it was too early for the wives to go out shopping. But as Tom slowed before his bungalow, he saw Harry Dylan, his nosy next-door neighbour, watering his lawn.

"Our luck!" he muttered under his breath.

Sheila got out of the car to open the double gates that led to their garage.

"Hello there, Mrs. Whiteside," Dylan shouted and turned off the hose. "Nice to see you. Did you have a good vacation? My! You certainly have picked up a sun-tan."

Harry Dylan was short, fat and balding. He had been a bank clerk and had now retired. He was always trying to get friendly with the Whitesides, who found him a bore, Tom suspected that he was infatuated with Sheila as Dylan seldom had anything to say to him when they ran into each other alone.

"Fine, thanks, Mr. Dylan," Sheila said and ran to open the garage doors.

"I see you have a new car, Mr. Whiteside. That's a much better job than your old one. When did you get that?"

Tom nodded to him and drove into the garage.

Dylan walked along the low fence and when he reached the Whitesides' garage, he leaned over the fence.

"It's not ours," Sheila said. "We had a breakdown . . . we had to borrow this to get back home."

"A breakdown! That's tough. Where did you get to?"

"All over." Seeing Tom was closing the garage doors, she said hurriedly, "Excuse me . . . we have to unpack," and she stepped back as Tom closed the second door.

"That guy!" he said angrily.

"Come on. Open up. Let's look."

Tom unlocked the boot and lifted the hood. He took out the gas cooker and set it on the floor. Sheila leaned into the boot and caught hold of the carton. She tried to drag it towards her, but found it was too heavy to move. She spun around.

"The money's in there! I can't move it!"

Tom began to shake.

"We could get into a load of trouble . . ."

"Oh, stop it! Help me!"

He joined her, and together they dragged the carton forward. As she began opening it, there came a knocking on the garage door.

They froze, looking at each other. Then feverishly, they shoved the carton back and closed the lid of the boot.

"Who is it?" Sheila asked breathlessly.

They walked slowly to the double doors and opened one of them. Dylan had come around the fence and grinned cheerfully at him.

"I don't want to disturb you, Mr. Whiteside, but while you were away the gas and electricity men called. I thought it neighbourly to pay the bills. Then there was a guy who said Mrs. Whiteside had ordered some cosmetics. I took in the parcel. Like to settle up now?"

Tom controlled himself with an effort. His smile was a grimace.

"We'll unpack first . . . thanks a lot. Suppose I come around when we've settled in?"

"Sure and bring your wife. Let's say in a couple of hours, huh? I'll open a bottle of Scotch someone gave me . . . it's damn fine Scotch if one can judge by its label. Like me to help you unpack? I'm pretty good at carrying things."

"No thanks. Okay, Mr. Dylan, in a couple of hours."

"That's right. Well, from the look of you, I guess you had a fine vacation. Did I tell you the wife and I are off next week? We're going to Lake Veronica. Should be some good fishing there. It will make a change. We haven't had a vacation for a couple of years."

Tom moved restlessly.

"Hope you have a good time . . . well, if you'll excuse me. We want to settle in."

"Why, sure. So you borrowed that car, huh? Nice one. I'd like to have a Buick."

"Tom!" Sheila's voice was shrill. "Will you come and carry this case?"

"There." Dylan's smile widened. "You and me talking, and the little woman does all the work."

Tom stepped back.

"Sure I can't help?" Dylan asked as the door began to close in his face.

"It's okay," Tom said and closed the door. He leaned against it, swearing under his breath. "One of these days, I'll kill that jerk!"

"Tom!"

He joined her as she opened the carton. The sight of the tightly packed wads of $500 bills made both catch their breath.

"Look at it!" Sheila whispered. "Oh, God! Look at it!"

With a shaking hand, Tom picked up one of the packets of money. Then as if it had bitten him, he dropped it back into the carton.

"We could get twenty years for this! We'd better call the police!"

Sheila took the packet he had dropped. With shaking fingers, she counted the bills.

"There's ten thousand dollars right here . . . *ten thousand dollars!*" She suddenly stiffened, threw the money back into the carton and faced Tom. "You fool! Oh, hell . . . how did I come to marry such a goddam dope?"

"What are you talking about? What do you mean?"

"You put our address on our car! That man could find our car and he'll know we have the money! Oh, God! How stupid can you be?"

"We're taking the money to the police," Tom said, speaking slowly and distinctly. "So, okay, let him know we have it . . . why should we care?"

"We're not taking the money to the police. Can't you ever

use that thing you call a head? If we turn the money over to the police, they will cash in on the reward! Have you ever had any reason to trust a cop? Come on, Tom, help me get this carton into the house. We've got to take this car back fast!"

"Take the car back? What do you mean?"

She turned on him, her eyes blazing and she slapped him heavily across the face, sending him reeling.

"Help me get this money into the house!" she said, her voice low and furious.

Her expression scared him. Muttering, unnerved, he dragged the carton out of the car. Together, they staggered with it into the living-room and dropped it heavily on the worn carpet. Sheila ran to the window and pulled down the blind.

"Come on! We'll get the pump and drive back. Every minute we waste could put us into worse trouble!"

He caught hold of her arm and jerked her around.

"What are you planning to do? What is all this?"

Her eyes glittering, her face white, she faced him.

"I'm handling this! You're going to do what I tell you! I've lived a year with you and I've had enough of your crummy way of life! Two and a half million dollars! We've got it! No one knows we have it. Now, listen to me . . . we're going to keep it! Do you hear me? We're going to keep every dollar of it!"

Maisky watched the Buick back out of the hide, turn and then drive down the short track to the dirt road. Two and a half million dollars! Going away from him after all his planning! He felt so bad he thought he was going to die.

He lay on the damp floor of the cave, his face resting on the back of his cold hand. He heard voices, then he heard the Buick drive away.

Who could these two be? he wondered. Why had they taken his car? They looked honest enough. Why had they taken his car?

He made the effort and sat up. They must have come in a car . . . where was it?

He stared down at the steep path that led from the cave to the glade. Then, moving aside the branches that covered the mouth of the cave, he started down the path, moving slowly, terrified that the pain in his chest might return.

Finally, he reached the glade. He looked around, then continued on down the path to the dirt road. There he saw a dusty Corvette Sting Ray under the trees and a slip of paper under one of the windscreen wipers. He approached the car and slid the paper from under the windscreen wiper.

He read Tom's message.

He closed his eyes and leaned against the car. So this was the explanation. They had broken down and had borrowed the Buick, but they were coming back! With any luck, they wouldn't look in the boot. How could they? They hadn't the key. Then he stiffened. The man had started the car . . . how had he done it, if he hadn't the key? That key would also open the boot! Well, maybe they wouldn't open the boot.

With a shaking hand he copied Whiteside's address down on the back of an old bill he had found in his pocket. Then he put Tom's note back under the windscreen wiper.

Well, now all he could do was to hope. They looked honest people. They would return the car, fix their own car and that would be the last he would see of them . . . with any luck. He hesitated, his cunning mind now very alert. Would they wonder what the car was doing in the glade? Would they report finding it to the police? Maybe he had better leave when they returned the car. But where could he go? He was now feeling weak and breathless again. He longed to lie down and rest. Moving cautiously, he made his way back to the cave.

Patrolman Fred O'Toole looked at his watch. In another ten minutes he would be off duty . . . and about time too! He had had more than enough of checking this continuous flow of cars leaving the City, and his temper was frayed.

Then he saw a car coming and he groaned to himself. He stepped out into the middle of the outward lane, holding up his hand.

The Buick coupe slowed and Tom Whiteside leaned out of the window. His face was pale under his sun-tan and his grin forced.

"Hi, Fred."

"Oh, you . . ." O'Toole looked puzzled. "I thought I saw you going home . . ." He came to the window and peered in at Tom and Sheila.

"Yeah . . . I'm now taking this car back," Tom said.

"Hello, Mr. O'Toole," Sheila said brightly. She gave him a sexy smile. "Long time no see. How do you like my sun-tan?"

O'Toole had always thought she was the most gorgeous piece of tail he had ever seen. He smiled at her, eyeing her breasts.

"You look good enough to eat, Mrs. Whiteside. Had a good time?"

"Did you ever take your wife on a camping vacation, Mr. O'Toole?"

O'Toole laughed.

"I don't look for trouble."

"Well, my love of a hubby doesn't know trouble when he sees it. But it wasn't all that bad."

In spite of the small talk, O'Toole didn't neglect to look the car over. He remembered the wanted car was a Buick coupe and this was a Buick coupe.

"Something new, Tom?" he asked.

"No . . . my goddam car broke down. I borrowed this. What's all the commotion about?"

"Commotion? Don't you read the papers? There's been a two-and-a-half-million-dollar steal from the Casino. We have the robbers holed up in the City so orders are to check every outgoing car."

"Is that right?" Sheila thrust her bust in O'Toole's direction. "Well, what do you know! Two and a half million . . . wheeee!"

O'Toole regarded her. Whiteside certainly had it good.

Imagine getting this frill into bed every night.

"I'll have to check the car, Tom," he said, getting back to business.

"Go right ahead." Tom gave him the ignition key. "I'm just returning this car and then picking up my own ruin."

O'Toole checked the boot, then gave Tom back the key. "Who did you borrow this from?"

"Oh, a guy . . . one of our clients," Tom said, flicking sweat off his face.

O'Toole leaned into the car and looked at the licence tag. Then he stepped back and wrote in his notebook: Franklin Ludovick, Mon Repose, Sandy Lane, Paradise City.

Tom watched him, feeling sick.

"Okay, go ahead. I'm off duty in five more minutes. Gee! Will I be glad!"

"I bet. Be seeing you," and Tom engaged gear and drove through the road block.

"Phew!" Sheila sighed softly.

Tom said nothing. He was thinking of the carton loaded with more money than he thought existed now in their sitting-room.

There must be a big reward, he thought. The insurance people would be covering the Casino. But it was a mistake not to go to the police right away. How could he explain the delay? He moved uneasily. He thought of what Sheila had said. She must be crazy! Glancing at her hard, cold face, he felt a prickle of fear. She couldn't really mean to stick to all that money!

He turned off the highway and began to drive up the dirt road.

"They could be there, waiting for us," he said suddenly.

"They? There's only one . . . he's over sixty and frail. You heard what was said on the radio," Sheila said scornfully. "Don't tell me you're scared of a man like that?"

But Tom was scared.

"This is out of our class. A man like that . . . he could have a gun."

"So what? So he has a gun . . . we have two and a half million dollars! If you can't handle him, I know I can!"

Tom moved uneasily.

"How you talk! Always the big mouth! I still think we should go to the police."

"Oh, for God's sake! We're not going to the police!"

They came within sight of the Sting Ray. He pulled up and got out of the Buick.

The note he had written was still under the windscreen wiper. He slipped it out and shoved it into his pocket. Well, he thought, beginning to relax, at least here's luck. This guy didn't find my car.

Going back to the Buick, he took out the new oil pump he had picked up at the G.M. garage and then set to work to change the dud for the new one.

Sheila walked into the glade and Maisky saw her. He watched her as she wandered around. In spite of his anxiety, his elderly lust was aroused. He eyed her heavy breasts and the slow roll of her buttocks as she walked.

This, he thought, could be one hell of a lay.

He was sorry when she went down the path on to the dirt road and he lost sight of her. He heard them talking, then a car started up. With a grinding roar and a rattle, the car moved off.

Maisky steeled himself, then walked down the path to the Buick. His hand was shaking as he unlocked the boot. He lifted the lid and then stood motionless. In a frenzy of sudden rage, he spat into the empty boot.

They had found and taken the carton!

Tom drove his car into the garage and cut the engine. Sheila slid out of the car and shut the garage doors. They walked quietly through the kitchen and then into the sitting-room. They stood looking at the carton, then Sheila lifted the lid.

"I never thought I would live to see so much money," she said huskily. Squatting down on her heels, she picked up one of the packets and pressed it to her breasts. "Two and a half million dollars . . . it's a dream!"

Tom dropped into a lounging chair. He felt shaky and scared.

"We can't keep it. We must tell the police."

She dropped the packet of money back into the carton.

"We are going to keep it . . . all of it." Going to the cocktail cabinet, she poured two big whiskies and gave him one. "Here . . ."

Tom swallowed the drink at a gulp. The spirit immediately hit him. He felt suddenly fine and a little reckless.

"No one knows we have it," Sheila said, sitting down and sipping her drink. "We must now use our heads. This is a gift . . . make up your mind about it. We are going to keep it."

Tom felt the whisky move through him.

"Okay . . . so suppose we are crazy enough to keep it? We can't spend it. Everyone knows in this goddam town that we never have any money. So what do we do with it?"

She looked thoughtfully at him, thinking this was a step in the right direction. At least he was becoming co-operative.

"We wait. In a few months' time it will be safe to move it out of here. They can't keep the road blocks going for ever. When things cool down, we'll blow."

Tom ran sweating fingers through his hair.

"So? What the hell do we do with this right now? Leave it here?"

"No . . . we'll bury it. That patch of ground under the kitchen window . . . we'll bury it there."

He stared at her, worried. She seemed to have an answer for everything.

"You realise we could go to jail for twenty years?"

"You realise we now own two and a half million dollars?"

Tom got to his feet. She was too strong for him. Maybe she could steer this thing right. He knew he was doing wrong, but even against his pricking conscience, the thought of owning all this money was too much for him.

"Okay. This is your funeral. I've got to go. Look at the time. I'm late already. What are we going to do with this box right now?"

Sheila hesitated, then said, "Let's put it in the spare bedroom. We can cover it with the eiderdown."

"If we are going to go through with this, you will be chained to this house. You can't go out. You realise this?"

"Do you think that's so rough? Keeping watch over this kind of money isn't a hardship."

"It could go on for months."

"So, okay. I'll stay right here for months."

He hesitated, then gave up.

"I still think we're playing this wrong. We should tell the police."

"I told you . . . I'm handling this. We don't tell the police."

He stared at her, then raised his hands helplessly. He knew he was being weak . . . stupid . . . but all this money . . .

"Well, all right."

"Let's get it in the bedroom."

They dragged the carton into their bedroom and pushed it against the wall. Sheila took the eiderdown off the bed and draped it over the carton.

"You get off. You'd better bring something in for supper."

Tom felt a sudden overpowering desire for her.

"If we are going through with this together," he said, his voice shaking and husky, "then we'd better go the whole way."

She recognised the despairing desire in his eyes and she once again recognised her complete power over him.

"Oh, well . . . if you must."

She slid down her slacks and stripped off her panties. Then she dropped back flat across the bed. When he thrust into her with desperate urgency, she clutched hold of him, making a response to please and control him. As he shuddered, clinging to her, she stared up at the fly-blown ceiling, so bored with him she could scream.

When he had gone, she took a shower. Then walking, naked, into the bedroom, she took the eiderdown off the carton and squatting on her heels, she spent a long time fondling the money.

Here, she thought, was power . . . the key to unlock the door that would lead into the world she had always dreamed about. Her first buy would be a mink coat, then a diamond necklace, and then every other jewel that caught her eye. She thought of a six-bedroom house with a bathroom to every bedroom, a vast lounge, a big garden, immaculately kept by Chinese labour. Then a maroon-coloured Bentley car and a Japanese chauffeur in a maroon-coloured uniform. There would be a motor-boat, of course: possibly a yacht. She wasn't sure about this as she had never been on the sea. She had it all planned: it was a dream she had had ever since she could remember. Well, now it was within reach.

She stood up, running her long fingers over her body, lifting her breasts, and sighing. Then she began to dress.

Somewhere along the line, Tom would have to go. He didn't fit in the picture. He was too small-time . . . . too narrow . . . too scared. She had in mind a dark, tall, well-built man who would know how to handle money, who would have the respect of head waiters, and who would know how to take care of a girl. Yes, some time in the future, she must lose Tom, but the time hadn't come yet.

Unable to resist the temptation, she took three-five-hundred-dollar bills from the carton, then she closed the lid and replaced the eiderdown. She slid the folded bills down the top of one of her stockings. It was exciting to feel so much money pressing against her skin.

She went to her wardrobe and regarded the contents with contempt. God! What a collection of ghastly rags! She put on a pleated grey skirt and a cream-coloured sweater.

Having done her face and hair, she walked into the sitting-room. She looked at her cheap wristwatch. It was a few minutes after eleven-thirty. Tom wouldn't be back until six. Usually, she went out, but now she found herself chained to the bungalow. There was nothing to read in the house. She frowned, suddenly realising that from now on until they left the bungalow for good she would be a prisoner here. With all that money to spend . . . what a waste of time!

She felt hungry and realised there was nothing to eat in the house. She hesitated, then getting up she called the Sandwich Bar at the end of the street. She ordered two chicken sandwiches and a bottle of milk. The man said he would send her order over right away.

She turned on the TV set, but at this hour the programme was so dull, she immediately turned it off. A boy arrived a quarter of an hour later with the food. She paid him, noting she had only three dollars and a few cents in her purse.

She ate the sandwiches while moving around the lounge. She was restless and kept thinking of all that money in the bedroom. She kept thinking what a waste of time it was to have to wait when she could now start a spending spree.

As she finished the last of the sandwiches, the front-door bell rang. The sound made her jump and she stood motionless, her heart hammering. Then, when the bell rang again, she went to the front door.

Harry Dylan was standing on the doorstep.

"I guess you forgot our little date," he said and waved a bottle of Old Roses at her. "The wife's gone shopping. I thought I'd look in."

She eyed him, hesitated, then decided he was better than boredom.

"Well . . . come in."

"Mr. Whiteside's gone to work, hasn't he?" Dylan was eyeing her figure. The tip of his tongue moistened his lips.

"Yes . . . he's gone to work."

She led the way into the sitting-room.

"Here are the receipts and the parcel."

She looked at the electricity and gas bills and tossed them on to the table.

"My husband will settle with these." She stared at Dylan. "He never leaves me any money."

"I guess most husbands are like that," Dylan said and laughed nervously. He couldn't keep his eyes to himself. "Well, how about a drink, Mrs. Whiteside?"

"Why not?"

She got glasses, charge water and ice. All the time she moved around, she was aware of his eyes on her body.

Well, let him look, the poor dumb fish, she thought. It's not costing me anything.

"You heard about the Casino robbery?" he asked, measuring out two big drinks. "Quite something. Two and a half million dollars! It's my bet they will never see that again!"

She sat down, deliberately careless with her skirt. She let him see the colour of her panties before she adjusted her skirt. He slopped some of his drink.

"Yes, I heard about it on the radio. What would you do with all that money, Mr. Dylan?"

"I wouldn't know . . . honestly. They say one man's got it now. I've worked in a bank for years, Mrs. Whiteside. I do know something about the value of money. Let me tell you . . . that's too much money. The average person wouldn't know what to do with it."

She had to make an effort not to show her contempt.

"Oh, I don't know. Money goes fast."

"But not as much money as that. It would be an embarrassment. And besides, it is all in $500 bills. Now, a bill that size creates suspicion. When I was at the bank and someone wanted to change a $500 bill, I always checked. Just imagine being landed with all those bills."

Sheila stared thoughtfully at her glass. She hadn't thought of this.

"Surely people do have $500 bills?"

"Of course, but not many of them. And the banks will now be watching for them." They sipped their drinks while his eyes ran over her legs. "So you had a good vacation?"

She didn't hear him. She was thinking . . . wondering whether a fat old fool like him knew what he was talking about. He probably didn't. After all, the rich gamblers at the Casino used $500 bills as she used lipstick.

"Mrs. Whiteside . . . you're day dreaming," Dylan said and laughed. "So far away . . . did you have a good vacation? Did you really enjoy it?"

Oh, God! Not that again! She was suddenly utterly

bored with him. She had hoped maybe he would help pass the time, but his obvious lust, his peeping eyes and his fat, sweating face now sickened her.

"Yes . . . fine." She finished her drink and stood up. "Well . . . sorry to push you out, but I have unpacking to do. Tom will settle up some time this evening. Thanks for the drink."

She got rid of him before he realised he was being bustled out. She watched him through the window as he walked away, looking lonely and depressed.

She grimaced.

Men! she thought.

eight

AT TWENTY minutes past midnight, Tom, who had been looking at his watch continuously for the past half hour, stood up.

"We can do it now," he said. "I'm not waiting any longer."

"Better go out and see if any lights are showing," Sheila said, but she too was anxious to get the money buried.

"I know . . . I know . . . you don't have to tell me!"

Tom went into the kitchen, turned off the light, opened the back door and walked into the garden.

It was a hot night, and there was a big moon like a dead man's face, casting a hard white light over the garden. He walked slowly down the garden path until he came to the bottom fence, then he turned and looked at the bungalows either side of his. They were all in darkness. He then hurried back as Sheila joined him.

"All right?"

"Yes . . . I'll get the spade. You go down to the fence and watch."

She nodded and moved past him.

The digging was harder than he imagined. They had left the flower bed empty, not bothering to plant it up, and the ground had turned hard.

Sheila kept coming up the path, asking if he wasn't finished, for God's sake. He snarled at her. Both of them were jumpy and their nerves were frayed.

Finally, he stepped out of the hole and peered down at it. It should be deep enough, he thought.

Seeing him get out of the hole. Sheila joined him.

"And hour and a half to dig a little hole!" she said scornfully. "What kind of man are you?"

"Oh, shut up!" Tom snapped. "The ground's like concrete. Come on . . . let's get the box."

They went into the bedroom where the carton was already wrapped in a big plastic sheet Tom had found in the loft. It was roped and ready to be buried. They dragged it out and dropped it into the hole.

"Go back and watch!" Tom said as he picked up the spade.

Twenty minutes later, they were back in their sitting-room. Tom poured himself a big shot of whisky. He was dirty, sweating and very jumpy.

"We're crazy to do this," he said, after a gulp at the whisky. "We'll never spend all that money! Why can't we settle for the reward?"

"So, okay, we're crazy," Sheila said. "Take a shower and go to bed. I'm sick of the sight of you!"

"Suppose someone digs it up while we sleep?"

"Who?"

"I don't know, but suppose . . ."

"So, okay, you want to sit up all night? Then go ahead."

He looked at her, exasperated.

"Some dog could . . ."

"Oh, quiet down!" She went into the bedroom and began to undress.

Tom hesitated, then he walked uneasily into the bedroom. After a hot shower, he felt more relaxed. As he came back into the bedroom, a quick, furtive move by Shelia arrested his attention.

"What are you up to?"

"Nothing."

"You were hiding something."

"Oh, be your age! I . . ."

He studied her, then walked over to her. She eyed him, tense, her eyes glittering. She was wearing a shortie night-dress that came well above her knees. He could see the pink of her nipples through the thin stuff.

As he reached to open the drawer of the chest by the bed, she slapped his hand away.

"Be your age, Tom!"

"Did you take any of the money?"

"No!"

"You're lying!" He gave her a hard shove that sent her flat on her back across the bed. Then he jerked open the drawer. But there was no money there.

She lay looking up at him, a sneering little smile on her lips, her shortie riding up way above her white thighs.

"Satisfied, caveman?"

He stood over her. His anxiety neutralised his sexual feelings.

"I don't trust you! You are money crazy! If you spend just one of those bills, we are cooked! Do you understand? Can you get this fact into your greedy mind? We don't touch any of that money until we are out of this State . . . can you understand?"

She sat up, holding the three $500 bills concealed in her right hand.

"You don't have to shout at me!"

"I'm telling you because you are greedy, stupid and bad. If we spend one of those bills . . . we're cooked!"

"I'm not deaf. I heard you the first time. What are you getting so worked up about? I haven't touched the money! Get into bed and stop acting like a B movie star."

She walked across the room into the bathroom, deliberately waving her hips at him. She kicked the door shut, then paused, listened and looked at the three crumpled bills in her hand. That had been a little close, she thought. If he had found them, he would have taken them from her. She hesitated, then hurriedly put the bills in a box of Kleenex which Tom never used. Then, humming under her breath, she took a shower.

Tom stretched out in bed. He thought of all that money outside in the garden. He thought of Sheila. She had been trying to hide something . . . he was sure of that. She was greedy and stupid enough to want to spend that money at once. He rubbed the side of his face, staring up at the ceiling. He must be mad to let her persuade him to keep the money!

She came into the bedroom and walked around the bed.

"I'll want some money tomorrow," she said, sliding under the sheet. "I have only three dollars."

"We'll have to watch it. I haven't much to last to the end of the month."

"Not much . . . only two and a half million dollars," and she laughed.

"How many more times do I have to tell you . . . we don't spend one dollar of that until we are out of the State!"

"I heard you the first time."

He snapped off the light. They lay in silence in the dark. Tom began to think how she had looked, lying across the bed with her shortie almost up to her navel. He began to move restlessly.

"Listen, Casanova," she said out of the darkness. "I recognise the signs. You've had your ration for the month. Go to sleep." She turned over, drawing up her long legs.

Neither of them slept much that night.

The sun coming through the branches that covered the mouth of the cave woke Maisky. He was immediately aware that he was feeling stronger. Suspicious, he lay still, staring up at the damp roof of the cave. Then he slowly sat up. He discovered he was feeling normal again and, startled, he got off the heap of blankets. He walked around the cave, stretching his thin arms.

The attack seemed over. Goddam it! He was actually hungry.

He cooked and enjoyed a breakfast of ham and eggs, washed down with weak coffee, then he shaved and washed in a bucket of water. He then sat on the bed of blankets, resting for twenty minutes, but he still felt perfectly normal. It was a miracle, he thought. The previous night, he thought he was going to die.

Soon his mind began to concentrate on the money. He would have to leave the cave. Those two might just possibly tell the police about the Buick, although he doubted it. They had taken the money so were they likely to alert the police? All the same, it would be risky to remain here and he never took risks.

He wondered where he should go, then he suddenly smiled. He took from his wallet the old bill on which he had written the address: *Tom Whiteside, 1123, Delpont Avenue, Paradise City*. What better place . . . where the money was?

He went over to the far end of the cave and squatted down before a shabby suitcase which he opened.

Maisky's years of associating with criminals had taught him to be always prepared for the unexpected. He had decided, long before the robbery, that there might come a time when he would have to drop out of sight. So he had come prepared. From the suitcase, he took out a thick, white wig, a black coat, black trousers, a black slouch hat and a clergyman's collar.

Ten minutes later, he was completely transformed. The small, frail, white-haired cleric who stared at his reflection in the hand mirror had no resemblance to Serg Maisky who had planned and executed the Casino robbery. He put on horn-rimmed spectacles, ran his fingers carefully through the false white hair, then put on the hat. He was sure he could walk past any policeman in perfect safety.

Then he packed the suitcase with the various things he would need, making it as light as possible. With a brief look around the cave, he walked slowly down the path and to the Buick.

He drove down the five miles of dirt road, stopped the car, parking it against a hedge. Then, carrying his suitcase, he walked slowly to the highway and to the bus stop.

"Don't go off without giving me some money," Sheila said as Tom put on his jacket.

"Come the time when you forget the word money . . . come the time." He gave her a five-dollar bill. "Nurse it. We're short. We could be in trouble at the end of the month."

"Come the time when we're not in trouble."

"I've got to get off. You stay right here, Sheila. I'll bring in supper."

"I'll stay."

When he had gone, she had a second cup of coffee, looked at her watch and grimaced. As it was only twenty minutes past eight, she went back to bed, but she was restless and couldn't sleep. She kept thinking of the three $500 bills in the Kleenex box. Finally, she got out of bed and took them from the box. Sitting on the edge of the bed, she examined each of them closely. They looked perfectly ordinary, but, not content with her scrutiny, she went into the sitting-room and found a magnifying glass Tom sometimes used to check small scale maps. Putting on the reading lamp, she went over each note under the glass. They were not marked, she decided. She was absolutely convinced of this . . . so why not spend them? She remembered what Dylan had said about the banks checking the big bills. Well, okay, she wouldn't go to a bank. Suppose she put a small bet on a horse and gave the bookie one of the bills? Bookies were used to handling $500 bills. They would give her change.

Pleased with this idea, she put the bills back in the Kleenex box and returned to bed. There was an all-night betting shop downtown. When Tom got back, she would say she had to have a breath of air and then go down there and place a bet.

Around eleven o'clock, having read the newspaper and getting bored with herself, she got up and dressed. She went into the kitchen, opened the window and looked down at the freshly turned soil of the flower bed. Tom had certainly made a mess on the path. It had been too dark for him to see it, but now, in daylight, it looked a real mess. She was wondering if she should go out and sweep up when she heard the front-door bell ring.

She stood motionless, alert and tense, then, when the bell rang again, she went to the front door. Her heart sank when she saw Harry Dylan standing there.

"Good morning, Mrs. Whiteside," he said cheerfully. "My word! Talk about energy! I see you've dug up your back bed. When did you do it . . . last night?"

Sheila kept her face expressionless with an effort although she could have killed this fat, little bore.

"Oh, that . . . Tom got a sudden bee in his bonnet. Yes . . . last night. He has too much energy."

"I was wondering when you were going to dig it up. It's a nice bed . . . a good size. I have a box of petunias I can spare. They would do well there."

"Thanks a lot . . . but Tom has his own ideas."

"What's he planning to put in? Geraniums would do well too."

"I don't know and I couldn't care less," Sheila snapped. "Excuse me. I have something on the stove," and she shut the door. She stood for a long moment, then drew in a deep breath. That creep! He never misses a thing, she thought.

She now decided against cleaning up the path. As Dylan had already noticed the digging why should she do a chore Tom could do when he got home?

She looked at her watch. Every time she looked at it, she thought of the gold watch with its circle of diamonds in Ashtons, the jewellers, downtown. She longed for it, and every time she passed the shop, she stopped to stare at it. It was so cute! To think Tom was that mean he wouldn't give it to her for their anniversary!

She shrugged. It was only half past eleven. The morning seemed endless. She went into the lounge, hesitated before the TV, then, deciding there couldn't be any programme to hold her attention, she dropped into a chair and lit a cigarette. She was now beginning to feel sorry that she had agreed to stay in the bungalow all day. It was all right for Tom. He was getting around, talking to people. But she was now in prison! But she knew she daren't go out . . . suppose someone . . . but who? She sat up, frowning. The money was buried. Who could possibly come here and dig up the garden? It was a ridiculous thought. She hesitated, then decided she would go out. At least, she could go to the Sandwich Bar and have lunch. That would make a change from sitting in this dreary hole all day. Yes, she would do that.

She went into the bedroom and changed her shoes. As she was getting her coat out of the closet, the front-door bell rang.

If it's Dylan again, I'll kill him! she thought and marched angrily down the passage and jerked open the front door. Then she stiffened, startled.

A small, slimly built clergyman stood on the doorstep. He was carrying a shabby suitcase and he looked at her, his grey eyes mild behind the lenses of his horn-rimmed glasses. His shock of white hair made two big wings under his black hat.

"Mrs. Whiteside?"

"Yeah, but I'm busy," Sheila said, curtly. "Sorry, we don't give to the church," and she began to shut the door.

"I have come about the money, Mrs. Whiteside," Maisky said gently. "The money you stole."

Sheila turned to stone. She felt the blood drain out of her face. The shock of his words made such a devastating impact on her, she thought she was going to faint.

He watched her reaction with a cruel little smile.

"I am so sorry to upset you like this." His cold, snake's

eyes moved over her body. "May I come in?" He moved forward, riding her back down the passage. He closed and locked the front door.

Sheila pulled herself together.

"Get out or I'll call the police!" she said huskily.

"That would be a pity, Mrs. Whiteside. Then neither of us would have the money. After all, there is enough for us to share . . . two and a half million dollars. Is this your living-room?" He peered into the room, then entered, setting down his suitcase. He took off his hat and walked over to the lounging chair, noticing with distaste the ash-trays spilling cigarette butts on to the floor, the used glasses standing on the sideboard, the film of dust everywhere and he grimaced. He had high standards of cleanliness. He decided this beautiful looking girl was a slut. "Do you mind if I sit down? I haven't been too well recently . . . exciting times." He looked slyly at her and laughed.

She stood in the doorway, watching him, wondering what she should do. He must be the fifth robber the police were looking for, but got up like this! A clergyman! Then she realised his cleverness. No policeman would give him a second glance.

"I don't want you here," she said, trying to steady her voice. "I know nothing about the money . . . now, get out!"

"Please don't be stupid." He crossed one thin leg over the other. "I saw you and your husband take my car. The money was in the boot. When you brought the car back, the money wasn't in the boot. So . . ." He lifted his hands. "I don't blame you for taking it. What have you done with it?"

"It's not here. I—I don't know what you are talking about."

Maisky studied her. She moved uneasily as their eyes met. She had never seen such malevolent eyes. They sent a chill through her.

"Mrs. Whiteside, when I play a rôle, I like to remain in character. At the moment, as you can see, I am playing the rôle of a kindly, harmless clergyman." He paused, then leaned forward, his face a sudden mask of terrifying, snarling fury. "You had better make sure I remain that way, you stinking whore, or I'll teach you such a goddam lesson you won't ever forget it!"

She was appalled at his viciousness and shrank back, her heart pounding. He stared at her, then relaxed. Suddenly he was mild and all smiles again.

"Do sit down, my pretty."

Unnerved, Sheila moved into the room and sat opposite him. She was really frightened. She felt this little horror would murder her at the slightest encouragement.

"What is your name?" he asked, mildly.

"Sheila." The word came reluctantly.

"A nice name." He put his finger tips together and peered at her over them, then he giggled. "You see, I am back in my rôle. Have you noticed the way clergymen use their hands? I should have been an actor. I watch people. I make a note of how they behave." He continued to smile his sly, cruel little smile. "But we were talking about the money. Where is it, my pretty?"

She thought of the soil on the garden path. He had only to look out of the kitchen window and he would know.

"We buried it in the garden last night," she said through dry lips.

"How clever of you! I think I would have done exactly the same." His eyes ran over her, lingered on her long legs, then he asked, "All of it?"

"Yes."

"Neither you nor your husband kept a few bills for your personal use?"

"No."

"Very sensible." He looked around the lounge and grimaced. "As I intend to stay here for a month or so, my pretty, I must ask you to keep the place cleaner. It is very sordid, don't you think? I am used to cleanliness."

Sheila felt blood rush to her face. Forgetting her fear of him, for this really touched her on the raw, she burst out,

"You go to hell. I don't want you here! I won't have you here!"

He regarded her, his snake's eyes suddenly cold.

"Oh . . . so you are still unco-operative?" He shook his head. "What a pity." His clawlike hand dipped into his pocket and he produced a small gun. He pointed it at her. Sheila drew in a hard, quick breath and pressed herself back against the chair. "Well now, my pretty, perhaps after all, I had better teach you a lesson. This little gun contains a strong acid. It is extremely effective at short range. It can peel the skin off your pretty face the way you peel an orange. Look . . ." He aimed the gun at her feet and squeezed the trigger.

A tiny cloud of white smoke appeared at her feet. When it had cleared, she saw with horror a small hole had been burnt in the carpet. She reared back as the fumes of the acid bit into the back of her throat.

Maisky chuckled.

"Impressive, isn't it? I suggest you keep this place cleaner in the future. Is that understood?"

She stared at him, unnerved, but furious. All right, you sonofabitch, she thought, you hold the cards now, but wait until it's my turn.

"Yes," she said.

"Good." Maisky dropped his gun into his pocket. "Let us now consider the situation. The police are hunting for me. This is an excellent hiding place. You are here to take care of me and the money is here . . . it is ideal. Now . . . you must have friends. Will they think it odd that you have a clergyman staying with you?"

"Yes."

"Of course . . . so we will have to find a reason why I am staying here. Now tell me, is your mother dead?"

"What has my mother to do with this?" Sheila demanded, startled.

"Come now, my pretty . . . I ask the questions . . . you answer them. That way we won't waste time. Is your mother dead?"

"Yes."
"Did she die here?"
"No . . . in New Orleans."
"Well, then, suppose I am the clergyman who buried her? I arrive here . . . you remember your dear mother . . . you offer me hospitality . . . I accept. What could be simpler?"
"My bitch of a mother dumped me when I was twelve!" Sheila said viciously. "I only know she died because a guy she two-timed too often cut her throat. It was in the paper!"
Maisky looked shocked.
"Who else knows this sordid tale?"
Sheila hesitated, then shrugged.
"Well . . . no one. If you think you can get away with it . . ."
"Then that's settled." Maisky looked at his watch. "It is nearly twelve. I am hungry. What have you to eat in this place?"
"Nothing."
He regarded her, his head slightly on one side.
"I had an idea you would say that. Well, then, go and buy something. A nice steak, a green salad and French fried potatoes would do very well."
"I can't cook," Sheila said sullenly.
His eyes moved over her body.
"That again doesn't surprise me, but I can. Go and get the food." He settled more comfortably in the armchair. "Are you good at anything, my pretty? Do you give your husband pleasure in bed?"
"Oh, go to hell!" Sheila went into the bedroom. She paused, then moved into the bathroom, shutting and locking the door. She took the three $500 bills from the Kleenex box and pushed them down the top of her stocking. Then she flushed the toilet, unlocked the door and, moving into the bedroom, she put on her coat.
Maisky was standing in the passage as she came out of the bedroom.
"Don't be long, my pretty. I'm hungry."

"I'll need some money. I have only five dollars."

"Let me have your bag."

She handed it to him, thankful she hadn't put the three big bills in there. He opened it, looked inside, then closed it. He took a fat wallet from his pocket and gave her ten dollars.

"A nice steak . . . the best . . . do you understand?"

She moved past him, opened the front door and walked down the path.

Tom Whiteside was trying without success, to sell a Buick Sportswagon to an elderly client. They were in the G.M. showroom, surrounded by cars and Tom was saying, "Look, Mr. Waine, you can't beat this model. Look at the size of it. With your family, it's dead right for the job."

Waine had listened to all Tom's sales talk and he was still unconvinced. Now, Tom was beginning to bore him.

"All right, Mr. Whiteside, thanks for your time. I'll think it over." He shook hands. "I'll talk to the wife."

Tom watched him walk out of the showroom and he swore under his breath. This is always happening, he was thinking. I get the jerks right up the dotted line and then they walk out on me.

Miss Slattery, who ran the office, called to him.

"You're wanted on the phone, Tom . . . your wife."

Tom stiffened. Now, what the hell? Was something wrong?

"I'll take it in my office," he said and hurried to his small box of a room and grabbed up the receiver. "Hello? Sheila?"

"Listen and don't talk," Sheila said. She was calling from a booth in a drugstore. Quickly, she told him about Maisky. Tom listened, stiff with alarm.

"You mean . . . he knows we have the money?" he said. "Judas! We'd better call the police!"

"Will you shut up and listen," Sheila said, her voice harsh. "There's nothing we can do . . . yet. We buried the money, didn't we? That makes us accessories. Tom . . . can you buy a gun?"

"A what?" Tom's voice rose a note.

"He has an acid gun. I don't trust him. We may even have to kill him," Sheila said. "We must have a gun."

"You're mad! Kill him? What are you talking about?"

"Can you buy a gun?"

"No! Of course I can't!"

"Yes, you can. Any pawnshop will sell you a gun. Bring it back with you!"

"But I haven't the money. Besides . . ."

Sheila drew in a long breath of exasperation.

"You cheap, useless fool! Well, come back as soon as you can," and she hung up.

"Sheila!" Tom jiggled the crossbar, then slammed down the receiver. His hands were shaking, his heart hammering. The intercom buzzed. For a moment he hesitated, then pulling himself together he snapped down a switch.

"Oh, Tom, here's Mr. Cain. He's waiting for his Caddy," Miss Slattery told him.

"Coming," Tom said and got to his feet.

What was Sheila talking about? Killing the man? Not quite knowing what he was doing, he walked into the showroom.

Sheila left the Paradise Self-Service store, carrying one of their blue-and-white plastic bags that contained a steak, a packet of frozen chips, a bag of beef sandwiches and a carton of ice cream. She walked quickly along the sidewalk, turned left down a narrow street and slowed. Ahead of her, she saw the three golden balls hanging outside Herbie Jacobs' pawnshop. She had been there several times when they had been so short of money they had had to pawn Tom's cuff-links and her gold bracelet that Tom had given to her for a wedding present. She opened the shop door and entered.

Jacobs came from an inner room.

"Ah, Mrs. Whiteside, it is indeed a pleasure." The little

man was wearing a skull cap. He stroked his greying beard as he beamed at her. What a beauty! he was thinking. What a lucky guy Whiteside was! Imagine going to bed with a beauty like this every night. Nothing to pay! His for the taking!

"I'm going on a trip, Mr. Jacobs," Sheila said, smiling at him. "I wonder if you can help me. Tom thinks I should have a gun. I'm driving . . . alone. Can I buy a gun from you?"

Jacobs stared at her, startled.

"Well . . ."

The pause hung for a long moment, then Sheila, aware of the passing time, said sharply, "Can I or can't I?"

"Yes, but guns aren't cheap, Mrs. Whiteside."

"I didn't think they would be. I want something small and not heavy."

"I have a .25 automatic . . . a beautiful little weapon," Jacobs said. "It costs a hundred and eighty dollars."

"Let me see it."

"If you don't mind coming into the other room . . . you understand? One has to be careful."

She followed him into the dingy inner room.

"Just one moment, please."

He went into another room and she could hear him rummaging about, muttering under his breath. Finally, he returned with a small gun in his hand.

"You understand guns, Mrs. Whiteside?"

"No."

"Of course . . . well, let me explain. Here is the safety catch. You pull it back . . . so. Be very careful: the trigger is light. It is an excellent gun. See . . ." He touched the trigger and she heard a sharp snapping sound. "Two hundred dollars, Mrs. Whiteside, and that includes ten rounds of ammunition . . . you won't need more?"

"No." She took the gun out of his grimy hand, balanced it and then pressed the trigger. Again she heard the snapping sound. Well, it wasn't complicated, she thought. "Will you load it, please?"

He regarded her, a little worried, a little puzzled.

"I will show you how to do it. It is better and safer for the gun to remain unloaded."

"Then it would be useless. Load it!"

He slid the cartridges into the clip and then inserted the clip into the gun, pressing home the spring. Then he put on the safety catch.

"You will be careful . . . accidents can happen." He paused, looking at her slyly, then went on. "You haven't bought this gun from me, Mrs. Whiteside. That is understood? By rights, I shouldn't be selling guns."

"Yes, I understand." She took the gun from him with four extra cartridges and put them into her bag. Then she gave him one of the $500 bills she had transferred from her stocking top to her bag during the bus ride down town.

He regarded the bill, his eyebrows crawling to the top of his forehead. She watched him, feeling tense and a little frightened.

"I will give you change. So Mr. Whiteside is having some success . . . I am so pleased."

"He sold three cars recently. About time . . ." She relaxed and followed him into the shop.

"Well, success finally comes. We all have to work for it . . . some are luckier than others." He gave her three one-hundred-dollar bills. "You should get a permit for the gun. I expect you know that. The police . . ." He waved his hand.

"I know . . . I'll see about it. Thank you, Mr. Jacobs."

Out on the street, she stood hesitating, then she turned and walked briskly to the main street. She walked into the Plaza Hotel and into the Ladies' room. Here, she locked herself in a toilet, took the gun from her bag and, lifting her skirt, she pushed the gun down the front of her girdle. The touch of the cold steel made her shiver. She lowered her skirt, smoothed the cloth over the slight bulge, then, taking from her bag the extra cartridges, she lifted the flush lid and dropped them into the water. Then she left the toilet and the hotel.

She walked down the street, feeling the gun chafing

against her skin. At the end of the street was a taxi rank. She headed towards it, then suddenly paused. She was right opposite Ashton's, the jewellers, and there was that gold watch beckoning to her. She hesitated for a long moment, then the thought of owning it overwhelmed her. She walked into the shop.

"Good morning, madame." The man behind the counter was tall, elderly and very refined. "Why, of course, it is Mrs. Whiteside. Your husband sold me a car last year. How is he?" As she stared blankly at him, he smiled, revealing plastic teeth. "I am Harold Marshall, Mrs. Whiteside. Your husband may have mentioned me."

This crummy town! Sheila thought. Like living in a fish bowl! She gave him a dazzling smile.

"Yes, of course. Mr. Marshall, it is our wedding anniversary next week. My husband wants me to have that gold watch . . . the one in the window."

"Now which one would that be?" Marshall said, going to the window and opening the grille.

She joined him and pointed.

"That one."

"Oh yes . . . it's quite the nicest design we have." He lifted the watch from its black-velvet bed. "It would make a splendid anniversary present. This is your first, I believe."

She wasn't listening, her eyes were on the watch.

"Let us try it on, Mrs. Whiteside."

She shivered as she felt the gold band grip her flesh. At last! Something she had longed for and dreamed about for months . . . now it was actually on her wrist!

"I'll take it."

He was slightly startled. She hadn't even asked the price! From what he had heard from the local gossip the Whitesides were always in debt.

"You couldn't do better, Mrs. Whiteside. I have a box."

"No, thank you. I'll wear it." She couldn't bear to be parted from the watch now she had it on.

"Of course. It is a self-winder. You will have no trouble, but if it gains a little bring it back. It will only need a small adjustment. You'll be happy with this for the rest of your life."

"I'm sure." She paused, staring fascinated at the watch, then, seeing he was becoming a little restless, she asked, "How much is it?"

He relaxed.

"One hundred and eighty dollars."

Well, she thought, I'm certainly spending money, and why not? Don't I own two and a half million dollars, but as she gave Marshall the second $500 bill, she thought of the little man waiting for her in the bungalow.

Then she became aware that Marshall was regarding the bill doubtfully.

"My husband made a killing at the Casino," she said hurriedly. "The first time he has ever won. Talk about luck! Two thousand dollars!"

Marshall smiled.

"Yes, indeed. You know, Mrs. Whiteside, although I admit I have often tried, I have never won a dollar at the Casino. I am very happy to hear Mr. Whiteside has been so fortunate."

"Yes."

He gave her change.

"Are you sure you don't want the box?"

"No, thank you . . . and thanks."

When she had gone, Marshall picked up the bill and frowned at it. He remembered the recent instructions he had received from police headquarters. A waste of time, he thought, but he wrote Sheila's name and address on the back of the bill before placing it in the till.

The time was twenty minutes to three. Tom Whiteside had been sitting at his desk, thinking of what Sheila had told him. The tension had become unbearable. He suddenly decided he must go home and find out what exactly was happening. Wiping his sweating hands, he got up and walked into the showroom.

Peter Cain, the head salesman, was talking to a client.

Tom could see Locking talking to someone on the telephone through the glass wall of his office. He hesitated, then, as Locking hung up, Tom walked uneasily to the door, knocked and entered the office.

Locking frowned at him.

"What is it, Tom? I'm busy."

White faced, sweat glistening on his forehead, Tom said, "I have to go home, Mr. Locking . . . something I ate. I feel terrible."

People who felt terrible bored Locking. He shrugged his fat shoulders.

"Okay, Tom, then get off," and he reached for a file of papers.

The unfeeling bastard! Tom thought as he walked to where he had parked his car. He got in, started the engine and drove fast down the highway.

Fifteen minutes later, his heart thumping, sick with apprehension, he drove into his garage and shut the doors. As he walked into the kitchen, he heard the TV was on. A voice, strident with excitement, was giving a commentary on a wrestling match.

He hesitated. What the hell was going on? As he moved down the passage, Sheila called softly to him from the bedroom. He found her sitting on the bed.

"Shut the door."

He did so, staring at her.

"What's happening? What . . . ?"

"He's a TV addict," Sheila said. "He's in there."

"He? Who?"

She clenched her fists with exasperation.

"The man the police are looking for . . . the fifth robber! I told you, you dope!"

"You really mean he's *here*? I thought you had gone crazy!" Tom stared at her, horror in his eyes.

"Must you always act like a brainless jerk?" Sheila said. "I told you . . . he found our address, thanks to you. He knows we have the money. He intends to stay here until it's safe for him to leave."

"He can't stay here!" Tom said wildly. "I'm going to call the police."

"You don't have to do that, Mr. Whiteside," Maisky said softly. He had opened the bedroom door so quietly neither of them had heard him come in.

Tom whirled around.

Maisky smiled at him. He wasn't wearing the white wig and he looked quite harmless in his clergyman's outfit until Tom looked into the grey snake's eyes and he flinched.

"I don't see what you have to worry about, Mr. Whiteside," Maisky went on. "There's enough money for all of us. Let's go into the living-room and discuss this quietly." Turning, he walked down the passage and into the living-room. A little reluctantly, he turned off the television, then sat down.

Tom and Sheila followed him, hesitated, then took chairs away from him. Tom stared at him, unable to believe this frail little man could be at the back of the Casino robbery, yet scared of him. Those eyes and the mild smile chilled him.

"Now . . . the money," Maisky said, placing his finger tips together. "I am quite happy to take one and a half million for myself. That leaves you two a million. I think that is fair. After all, I engineered the plan. I shall have to remain here for a few weeks, but this I have already discussed with Mrs. Whiteside. You are being well paid for putting up with me. Do you accept these terms?"

There was a pause, then, as Tom was hesitating, Sheila said, "Yes . . . all right."

She was thinking if this little freak imagined he was going to walk out of here with a million and a half dollars, the joke would be on him. She thought of the .25 automatic she had hidden. When the time came for him to leave, he would walk into one hell of a surprise.

Tom stared at her.

"We can't agree!" he exclaimed. "We're not keeping a dollar of the money! We could go to jail for twenty years! I've had enough of this! I . . ."

"Will you shut up, you gutless ape!" Sheila screamed at him. Her fury was so violent, it silenced him.

Maisky giggled.

"And they call women the weaker sex," he said. "Well now, my pretty, so we are agreed?"

"You heard me, didn't you?" Sheila snapped at him.

Maisky smiled, his eyes glittering. She's dangerous, he thought, and greedy. Well, if she imagined she was going to get a cent out of this, she needed to have her pretty head examined. All the same, he would have to watch her.

"Fine." He appeared to relax. "Now that's arranged and we don't have to worry our heads further about it, perhaps I could go on watching the wrestling. It amuses me." He got up and turned on the TV set. "A wonderful invention, Mr. Whiteside . . . a great time-passer."

Tom got up and walked stiffly into the kitchen.

As the strident, excited voice of the commentator began to fill the room, Maisky dismissed Sheila with a wave of his hand.

"Run along, my pretty," he said. "I am sure this must bore you."

She stared at him, then got up and joined Tom in the kitchen.

"Any coffee left, Chief?" Beigler asked, lighting a cigarette from the stub of another. He leaned back in his chair, his heavy frame making the chair creak.

"There's a drop," Terrell said and pushed the carton across the desk. "You smoke too much, Joe."

"Yeah." Beigler poured coffee into the paper cup. "That's always been my trouble." He drank the coffee and then picked up the long typewritten report that had come from the road blocks. It contained a twenty-page list of car numbers and car owners who had passed through the road blocks on their way out of town. "This is getting us nowhere fast."

"Keep at it," Terrell said. "We're gaining some ground. We now know where he hired the truck and the trucker has a good description of him. When we catch up with him, we have him for sure."

"We haven't caught . . ." Then Beigler paused, stared at the list he was holding and stiffened. "Hey, Chief! Look at this!" He passed the sheet to Terrell, his thumbnail underscoring the typewritten line.

Terrell read *Franklin Ludovick, Mon Repos, Sandy Lane, Paradise City. Lic. No. P.C. 6678.*

"Whose report?"

"Fred O'Toole."

"Get him here!"

Beigler called down to Charlie Tanner.

"We want Fred. Is he at the road block still?"

"Hold it." There was a pause, then Tanner said, "No. He's back home. Clocked off half an hour ago."

"Get him. Send a car, Charlie . . . pronto."

"Will do," Tanner said and hung up.

Twenty minutes later, Patrolman Fred O'Toole walked into Terrell's office. He was out of uniform and showed signs of having scrambled into a pair of slacks and an open-neck shirt.

"Come in, Fred," Terrell said, waving to a chair. "Sorry . . . I guess you were putting your feet up."

"That's okay, sir," O'Toole said, stiffly at attention. It was all right for the Chief to be friendly, but Beigler was his boss.

"Sit down," Terrell said. "Don't we have any coffee in this place?"

Beigler grabbed the telephone. He told Tanner to send out for coffee.

"What again?" Tanner said wearily.

"You heard me," Beigler said and hung up. "Relax, Fred."

Uneasily, O'Toole sat on the edge of a chair.

"Fred . . . this Buick coupe. Owner, Franklin Ludovick," Terrell said, passing the typewritten sheet across the desk. "What can you tell me about it?"

"It came through the road block as stated, sir. It was driven by Tom Whiteside, the G.M. agent."

"Dr. Whiteside's son?"

"That's correct, sir."

"Go on."

"He said he had broken down and had borrowed the car from a client."

Terrell and Beigler exchanged glances.

"Did you check the car, Fred?"

"Not on the inward trip, sir. We weren't checking incoming cars, but a couple of hours later, he came back. He said he was returning the car. I checked it then. It was clean."

"Was he on his own?"

"His wife was with him."

Terrell thought for a moment, then nodded.

"All right, Fred, you get back home. Have them drive you back."

When O'Toole had gone, Terrell got to his feet. Beigler was already putting his .38 into its holster. He then snatched up the telephone receiver and told Tanner that Jacoby and Lepski were to report to the car pool pronto.

"I've got your coffee," Tanner said.

"Drink it for me," Beigler said and hung up.

He followed Terrell down to the car pool. As they got into a police car, Lepski and Jacoby came running down the ramp. They scrambled into the back as Beigler set the car in motion.

Terrell explained the set-up to them.

"You two cover us. Lepski: take care of the back. Watch it! Could be a tricky one. We'll play it by ear."

Ten minutes later, the car pulled up outside the Whitesides' bungalow.

Terrell and Beigler walked up the path and rang on the front-door bell.

nine

TOM WHITESIDE had just finished sweeping the soil off the garden path when he saw Detective 2nd Grade Lepski appear in the lane at the bottom of his garden. He recognised him immediately. Lepski was a well-known character in Paradise City. The sight of him made Tom's heart skip a beat. Looking quickly away from the detective, he leaned the broom against the wall and walked into the kitchen.

In the living-room, Maisky saw the police car pull up and Terrell and Beigler start up the path.

"It's the police," he said quietly to Sheila. "Now, don't lose your head. Remember I am Father Latimer from New Orleans. It's going to be all right if you handle it right."

His calm, confident tone quietened Sheila's momentary panic.

As the front-door bell rang, Maisky went on, "Let them in. Act naturally and relax."

He sat down in a lounging chair after a brief glance in the mirror over the mantelpiece to make sure his wig was on straight.

Her heart pounding, but her face composed, Sheila went to the door and opened it.

"Mrs. Whiteside?" Terrell said, although he knew her all right. There were few residents of the City who didn't know her by sight.

"Why, yes." She forced a smile. "It's Chief of Police Terrell, isn't it?"

"Yeah . . . Mr. Whiteside in?"

"Yes. He came home early. He isn't very well . . . something he ate, but do come in."

She led him and Beigler into the living-room. Both the police officers were startled to see a small, white-haired clergyman sitting quietly in an armchair. Maisky got to his feet, his smile bright with welcome.

"This is Father Latimer from New Orleans," Sheila said. "He is staying with us. Father, this is Chief of Police Terrell and—and . . ." She looked at Beigler, flashing him a smile.

Some chick! Beigler thought as he introduced himself. He had trouble keeping his eyes from those long, slim legs.

"Yes . . . well, do sit down. I'll fetch Tom."

She left the room. Maisky shook hands with Terrell and then Beigler.

"I am happy to know you," he said. "This is my first visit to your beautiful City." His expression became solemn. "I had the unhappy task of laying Sheila's mother to rest."

Terrell moved uneasily and muttered something under his breath. There was a pause, then Tom came into the room with Sheila at his heels. He was white faced and sweating.

"Hello, Chief," he said. "You—you wanted me?"

"I hear you're not well," Terrell said, eyeing him. He certainly didn't look well.

"Something I ate . . . I'll be okay," Tom said. "Either of you two gentlemen care for a drink?"

"No, thanks . . . Mr. Whiteside, this Buick coupe you were driving . . ."

Maisky had sat down. He pressed his finger tips together and beamed at the others.

"Buick?" Tom said stupidly.

"Oh, Tom . . . we shouldn't have taken it!" Sheila exclaimed. She was now in control of herself. "You know, I said we shouldn't."

Tom gaped at her, then desperately trying to control his jumpy nerves, said hurriedly. "Yeah . . . that's right."

Terrell stared at him, then at Sheila, then back to Tom. "Mr. Whiteside, we have reason to believe the car belonged to one of the Casino robbers. Suppose you tell me how you came to be driving it?"

Sheila caught her breath dramatically and clapped her hands. Watching her, Maisky hoped she wasn't going to overplay her act.

"So that's why it was hidden!" she exclaimed. "Tom! And we took it! We hadn't an idea!" She turned to Terrell, her big eyes wide. "Of course . . . that explains it, and there we were thinking it belonged to some hunter . . ."

Terrell regarded her.

"Suppose you start this from the beginning," he said.

"Of course. Please sit down." She dropped into an easy chair, letting Beigler get a glimpse of her thighs as she adjusted her skirt. "We were coming back from a camping vacation. It was late. Tom decided to take a short cut from the Miami highway, down the dirt road through the woods, to the Paradise City highway. I'm sure you must know it . . ." She broke off, seeing Terrell was still standing. She was determined to dominate the interview, and smiling, she pointed to a chair. "Do please sit down, Chief. You look so tall, standing like that."

Terrell lowered his bulk into a chair while Beigler, notebook in hand, leaned up against the wall. Tom sat on an upright chair, behind Sheila.

"This is all news to me," Maisky burbled. "I have only just arrived. Has there been a robbery, then?"

"Excuse me," Terrell said curtly. "I want to hear what Mrs. Whiteside has to say."

"I'm sorry . . . of course . . . excuse me." Maisky beamed, settling himself back in his chair. "This is all very interesting."

Well, at least, I have got it away from that numbskull, Sheila was thinking, and I've got to keep it away from him.

"Yes," she said, leaning forward and staring with round eyes at Terrell. "So we took this dirt road and then our car broke down. It was the oil pump, wasn't it, Tom?" She looked over her shoulder. "You said it was the oil pump?"

Tom jerked his head.

"That's right."

"Well, there we were . . . right in the middle of the forest . . . stuck, and it was growing dark." She crossed her legs for Beigler's benefit. May as well give this flatfoot something to concentrate on, she thought. Beigler, who never missed anything like that, thought she was sensational . . . and those legs! "We decided to sleep the night there. In the morning as we were getting ready to walk . . ." She paused to make a comic gesture. "Imagine walking five miles! I found this car." She regarded Terrell to see how he was accepting her story. No good flashing her sex at him. He was one of the square, safely married fossils.

"When you found the car, Mrs. Whiteside, didn't you think you should have reported it to the police?" Terrell said.

She laughed.

"I just didn't think . . . nor did Tom. We were worried about leaving the camping equipment in our car. We had borrowed it and it could have been stolen while we were walking down to the bus stop. I just refused to be left alone in that forest . . . it scared me." She paused and looked at Beigler, inviting his sympathy. He thought: I'd like to have you alone, baby . . . a desert island for preference. She switched her gaze back to Terrell. "So we didn't think. Tom had a master key. We put our things in the car and took off. As soon as we got home, we unpacked, then got a new pump and went back. We left the Buick right where we found it. Tom fitted the new pump and we drove home."

Terrell scratched the side of his jaw. This sounded like the truth, he thought. O'Toole's report jelled with hers.

"Did you look in the boot?" he asked Tom.

Tom started, hesitated, then shook his head.

"Why, no. We—we just threw our stuff on the back seat. No . . . we didn't look in the boot."

Terrell got to his feet.

"I'll have to ask you to show us where you left the Buick . . . right now."

"Of course." Tom got to his feet. "I'll just put on my jacket."

As he left the room, Sheila stood up.

"You really mean, Chief, that we were driving the gangster's car?"

"I guess so," Terrell said, aware that Beigler's eyes were roving over Sheila's body.

"Well!" Sheila spun around to Maisky who was now standing. "I guess we'll be able to eat out on this story for weeks!"

"Quite extraordinary," Maisky said. "But I don't understand what it is all about." He peered at Terrell. "Why do you imagine the car was hidden, Inspector?"

Terrell muttered something, then walked to the door. This little, white-haired clergyman bored him.

Tom came out of the bedroom. His white, drawn face sent a pang of fear through Sheila. The dope could yet spoil everything, she thought.

"All set, Chief," Tom said.

Sheila ran to him and kissed his cheek—something she hadn't done for as long as he could remember. Then, with a wifely gesture, she straightened his tie.

"You won't keep him long, Chief," she said to Terrell. "He really is sick, but he's being awfully good about it."

"We won't be long, Mrs. Whiteside."

Terrell opened the front door, then, followed by Tom Beigler, went down the garden path.

Sheila stood in the doorway and watched the three men get in the car. Then Lepski came down the road and joined them. As he slid under the wheel, Jacoby squeezed in at the back.

The car drove away.

"Very nicely done, my pretty," Maisky said as Sheila came into the living-room. "I couldn't have done better myself."

She ignored him. Going to the cocktail cabinet, she poured out a stiff gin and drank it. Then shuddering, she put down the glass.

"Just as long as that fool doesn't make a mistake," she said more to herself than to Maisky, then she went into her bedroom and slammed the door.

As the police car reached the path leading to the glade, Tom said, "This is it. Up that path . . . that's where I left the car."

Lepski pulled up. He, Jacoby and Beigler spilled out of the car, drawing their guns, leaving the car doors hanging open. They started up the path, moving cautiously.

Terrell got out, gun in hand.

"Stay right here, Mr. Whiteside," he said. "This guy could be around, and he's dangerous." He followed the others up the path.

Tom took a pack of cigarettes from his pocket. His hands were shaking so badly, he had trouble lighting his cigarette, but he was feeling more confident. The drive from the bungalow had been better than he had imagined it would be. Going with these policemen had given him, at first, the nightmare feeling of being arrested but, as it turned out, it wasn't like that at all.

About the first words Terrell had said as the car moved off were, "I knew your dad . . . a fine man . . . I would say, he was the finest man we have ever had in this City. He took care of Carrie . . . that's my wife . . . when she was in real trouble. You have nothing to worry about. These things happen."

Tom recalled his father. He must have been a very special type of man, he thought, and yet I never realised it. It's only when people as old as Terrell talked about him, he comes alive, and yet he was always decent to me . . . decent and understanding. I was just too goddam dumb to appreciate him. He dragged hard on his cigarette. He thought of all that money buried in the garden. He must have been out of his mind to let Sheila dominate him. He should have told the police the moment he had found the carton in the boot. He moved uneasily. It was too late now. Well, he now made up his mind. He wasn't going to touch a dollar of that money. Sheila could take it all, and she could clear out. He drew in a long, deep breath. What a relief it would be to be rid of her! The past year had been the unhappiest he had ever lived through. Let her take the money and go!

Ten minutes later, Jacoby came running down the path. He grabbed the telephone receiver in the car and started talking to headquarters.

"We want Hess here and the squad," he said. "The dirt road between Miami and the City's highway. Hurry it up!"

He then went back up the path. Tom continued to sit in the car. He smoked four cigarettes and waited another fifteen minutes before Terrell appeared.

"The Buick's not there," Terrell said. "You are sure you left it in the glade?"

Tom stiffened.

"Yes, Chief. That's where we left it."

"We've found his hideout . . . a cave, but no car."

"That's where we left it."

Two police cars came bumping down the dirt road and pulled up. Hess and his squad spilled out.

"Go ahead, Fred. We've found his hide-out," Terrell

pointed to the path. "Get your men working on it."

Beigler, lighting a cigarette, joined Terrell.

"We'll drive to the highway," Terrell said. They got in the car, Terrell sitting beside Tom. Five miles fast driving brought them to the parked Buick.

"Well, here it is," Terrell said. They all got out and walked to the car. Beigler tried to open the boot, but it was locked. He looked at Tom. "Can you open it?"

Tom nearly fell for this, but at the last split second, his mind became alive and he shook his head.

"I have an ignition key, but not the key to the boot."

Beigler stared at him, then went to the police car, got a tyre lever from the tool box and returned to the Buick. He wrestled for a long moment, before he broke the lock. He lifted the lid of the boot.

"Nothing," he said and then looked at Terrell. "Could be he swopped cars again, Chief."

"Okay, Joe. Let's get back to headquarters. We can drop Mr. Whiteside on the way."

They got in the police car and Beigler sent it shooting along the highway.

"Maisky could have stashed the carton some place before he moved into the cave," Terrell said, speaking his thoughts aloud. "We know he couldn't have got the carton past the road blocks, but he's a bright boy. It is just possible he has hidden the carton somewhere and has got out. That sum of money is worth waiting for. He might be prepared to wait six months before coming back here and collecting the money."

Beigler grunted. "We must be sure no one answering his description has left town without the carton."

"More work," Beigler said. "Where could he hide a box that size?"

"Any left-luggage office for a start. But he couldn't have handled it on his own. We'll get it on TV and the radio. Someone might have spotted him."

Tom listened to all this, realising that these two didn't

even suspect him of having the money. This was something, he thought, he found hard to believe, until he again thought of his father. It was his father as usual who gave him his background of respectability. Even from the grave, his father was casting a cloak of protection around him and Tom felt ashamed.

They pulled up outside his bungalow.

"Okay, Mr. Whiteside. Thanks for your help," Terrell said. "We won't bother you now. Tomorrow, I'll want a statement from you." He regarded Tom's white, strained face. "I guess you should get to bed."

"I think I'll do that," Tom said. "Whatever I ate is playing hell with me."

As the police car drove away, Sheila opened the front door. Maisky was standing in the living-room doorway. Both of them were very tense.

"Well?" Sheila asked as Tom came up the path.

"It's okay so far," Tom said, moving past her. To Maisky, he went on, "They think you have hidden the carton somewhere and have left town."

Maisky smiled.

"Suppose we all have a cup of tea?" he said. "Get us some tea, my pretty. There is nothing like tea when you have had a shock."

To Tom's surprise, Sheila went into the kitchen and put on the kettle.

"We'll get away with this," Maisky said, sitting down and pressing his finger tips together. He beamed at Tom. "I have a feeling about it. You see . . . we'll get away with it."

Tom went into the bedroom. He kicked off his shoes, shed his jacket and dropped flat on the bed. He felt cold and sick. He lay back and closed his eyes.

Later, he heard Sheila go into the sitting-room and the chink of tea cups. She came to the bedroom door.

"Do you want tea?"

Without opening his eyes, he shook his head.

"Just leave me alone . . . will you?"

"Don't act like a goddam prima donna!" Sheila said furiously. "Pull yourself together! Don't just lie there!"

He opened his eyes and stared at her. How could he have possibly loved this woman? he thought. He sat up and swung his legs off the bed.

"I want you to get out of here as soon as it is safe to move the money," he said. "I've had enough of you. Take the money . . . take that little ape with you, but get out and leave me alone! I'm not touching a dollar of that money! Do you hear! All I want is to see the last of you!"

She stared at him, startled, then she threw back her head in a strident laugh.

"Mr. Cheapie to the end. Do you imagine I don't want to see the last of you, you poor creep? Okay, if that's the way you want it, it suits me fine. When our little pal thinks it is safe to go, I'll go too, but not before."

Maisky listening to this smiled. Well, he thought, at least I now don't have to worry about the man. All I have to do is to watch this bitch.

He nipped back to his chair as Sheila came down the passage.

"Your tea is getting cold, my pretty," he said. "Did I hear you two arguing about something?"

"Mind your own business!" Sheila snapped, taking her cup of tea. She walked to the window and stared out, her mind busy.

Maisky stared at her, then shrugged. He walked to the TV set and turned it on.

"Oh, give it a rest, can't you?" Sheila said without turning.

"Certainly not." Maisky consulted his watch. "It is time for the news. In our situation, my pretty, it is always well to keep up with the news."

Halfway through the programme, the announcer said, "We have several items of news concerning the Casino robbery. As we announced last night, the police are still warning all banks and shops to look out for any $500 bills that might be offered for change. These bills must not be accepted unless the person offering them is known and the name and address of the owner written on the bill. The police are also . . ."

Sheila dropped her cup. It fell on the parquet floor, spilling the hot tea and smashing into pieces. Slowly, she put down the saucer, a cold fear gripping her heart.

Marshall . . . the watch! Had he put her name on the bill she had given him? *Had he?*

At the sound of the smashing cup, Maisky jerked around in his chair. He saw her expression of fear, the tightness of her mouth, her scared, glittering eyes and he knew at once she had spent one or more of the bills.

He remained motionless for a long second, his face convulsed with rage, then, feeling his heart begin to hammer, he got slowly to his feet.

"You bitch!" he said, his voice strangled. "You've spent some of the money . . . haven't you?"

Sheila stepped back, shaken by the vicious expression on his thin face. He was suddenly transformed into a deadly wild animal.

"No!"

"You're lying! You spent some of that money!"

"I tell you I didn't!"

He left the room, moving swiftly, and burst into the bedroom where Tom was lying on the bed.

"Get up! Your whore has spent some of the money! What could she have bought?" Maisky's voice was shrill with rage. "Search the place! She's spent some of the money!"

With a feeling of dread, Tom got off the bed.

"She couldn't have . . . she's not that stupid," he said.

Maisky glared around the room, then he rushed to the chest of drawers and pulled out the top drawer. The drawer fell to the floor and Maisky, muttering, half insane with rage and fear, upended it.

The .25 automatic and the gold watch came into sight from between a pair of blue panties and a bra.

Beigler poured coffee into two paper cups. He passed one cup to Terrell, and then carried the other to his desk.

"Look, Chief," he said as he sat down, "have you thought the Whitesides could have found the money and are sitting on it?"

Terrell sipped the coffee and then began to load his pipe.

"Not Tom Whiteside, Joe. We have to keep this thing in the right perspective. I've known his father for years . . . he was a saint."

"Does that make his son a saint?" Beigler asked patiently.

"All right, Joe . . . it doesn't, of course, but he's not the type. For one thing, he wouldn't know what to do with all that money."

"But his wife would."

Terrell scratched the side of his jaw and frowned at Beigler.

"No, it still doesn't add up. It's my bet Maisky had another car. He moved the carton into this car, leaving the Buick. I think he's hidden the carton somewhere and has left town. He'll come back in three or four months."

"Where do you imagine he has hidden the carton that size?" Beiger asked.

"Could be anywhere . . . the beach . . . a left-luggage office . . . any damn place."

Beigler sipped his coffee and rubbed the end of his thick nose. Watching him, Terrell recognised the signs, then he said, "The boot was locked, Joe." He was reading Beigler's mind. "Neither of the Whitesides could know the carton was in the boot."

Beigler picked up the telephone receiver.

"Charlie? Get me Mr. Locking of General Motors."

Terrell put down his cup of coffee and regarded Beigler with worried eyes.

There was a short delay, then Beigler said, "Mr. Locking? This is Sergeant Beigler, City Police. Sorry to bother you, but I have a little query you could help me with. With a Buick coupe, can the ignition key open the boot or do you have to have a separate key?" He listened, then said, "Thanks, Mr. Locking . . . much obliged," and hung up. He looked at Terrell. "The ignition key can open the boot of a Buick coupe, Chief."

Terrell sat back.

"Whiteside said it couldn't?"

Beigler nodded.

"That's what he said."

They looked at each other, then Terrell pushed back his chair and stood up. As Beigler once again slid his .38 into its holster, the telephone bell rang. Impatiently, he snatched up the receiver.

"The Head Teller of the Florida Bank is asking to speak to the Chief," Tanner told him.

Beigler passed the receiver to Terrell.

"For you, Chief. The Florida Bank."

"Yes?"

"Chief, this is Fabian, Florida Bank. We have one of the marked $500 bills just come in from Ashton, the jewellers. The name on the bill is Mrs. Whiteside, 1123, Delpont Avenue."

Terrell looked over at Beigler, then asked, "You're sure it is one of the marked bills?"

"I'm sure."

"Thanks, Mr. Fabian. Keep the bill for me, please," and he hung up. "Get Lepski and Jacoby," he went on to Beigler. "You're right on the target, Joe. She's already spent one of the bills. Let's go."

"I'm still on the target," Beigler said. "That little runt . . . Father Latimer. Is it likely people like the Whitesides would have a clergyman shacked up with them . . . could be Maisky."

Terrell suddenly grinned.

"The trouble with you, Joe, is you're getting too smart. Come on, let's go."

Seeing the .25 automatic on the floor, Maisky bent and grabbed at it. Tom struck it out of his hand. The gun fell between them. Cursing, Maisky again bent to grab it, but Tom kicked it under the bed.

"Cut it out!" he said.

Maisky straightened. He glared at Tom, his eyes wild.

"Yes . . . I have something better than that for that whore!" As he made to leave the room, Tom grabbed him by his shoulder and whirled him around.

"I said . . . cut it out!"

Maisky's face worked convulsively.

"Do you think I'm going to let that bitch get away with this?" he shrilled. "The plan of a lifetime . . . two and a half million dollars, and because of her goddam greed, she queers it! I'll strip the skin off her face." His clawlike hand slid into his pocket and he pulled out the acid gun.

Tom hit him hard on the side of his jaw, grabbing the gun out of his hand at the same time.

There seemed to be an explosion inside Maisky's chest. He fell on his knees. The pain for a brief, dreadful moment was beyond his endurance. Although he tried to scream, no sound came. Then darkness folded in on him and there was nothing. He flopped limply face down on the floor.

Sheila came to the doorway. She looked at Maisky's body, then at Tom. Her face was white and granite hard.

"I'm pulling out," she said. She saw the gold watch on the floor and snatched it up.

Tom gripped her wrist and wrenched the watch out of her grasp.

"Get out!" he said. "You're not taking this! This goes to the police!"

She drew back regarding him, her smile sneering and contemptuous.

"You poor sucker," she said, "will you never learn?"

Turning, she went into the passage, then hesitated. Her mind was working fast. She had eleven hundred dollars . . . not much. She wondered if that little freak had any money. She ran into the second bedroom. His shabby suitcase stood against the wall. She put it on the bed and snapped back the clips. She found no money in the suitcase, but there was a jar of *Diana* hand cream amongst his dirty shirts. *Diana* hand cream! for God's sake, she thought. It cost $20 a jar! What could a little creep like him be doing with this! She dropped it into her handbag.

Well, she thought, with eleven hundred dollars, I'll get by. I came to this goddam City with nothing . . . at least, I am leaving with something.

She went into the tiny hall and snatched up her coat. There was a Greyhound bus due in five minutes. She could just make it to Miami. Once there, she could drop out of sight. She started for the front door.

"Sheila!"

She paused and looked at Tom as he stood in the doorway.

"I'm going . . . so long, Cheapie, and thanks for nothing," she said and jerked open the door.

"He's dead," Tom said. "Do you hear? He's dead!"

"What do you expect me to do . . . bury him?" Sheila asked and started down the path.

She half ran, half walked towards the bus stop, carrying her death in her handbag.

THE END

DO ME A FAVOUR, DROP DEAD
by James Hadley Chase

Keith Devery arrived in the small town of Wicksteed with a criminal record and a lot of ambition. And when he met Frank Marshall, a local drunk who was about to inherit a million dollars, he knew that here was a golden opportunity to get back into the big league. Marshall's mysterious wife Beth agreed with him . . . and together they ruthlessly plotted the perfect murder. Then Keith found that he had himself been set up . . . and that Beth had plans of her own once the money was hers . . .

'The thriller maestro of the generation'
Manchester Evening News

0 552 10574 0 £1.50

NO ORCHIDS FOR MISS BLANDISH
by James Hadley Chase

When Dave Fenner was hired to solve the Blandish kidnapping, he knew the odds on finding the girl alive were against him – the cops were still looking for her three months after the ranson had been paid. And the kidnappers, Riley and his gang, had disappeared into thin air. But what none of them knew was that Riley himself had been wiped out by the rival gang – and the heiress was now in the hands of Ma Grisson and her son Slim, a vicious killer who couldn't stay away from women . . . especially his beautiful new captive. By the time Fenner began to close in on them, some terrible things had happened to Miss Blandish . . .

One of the classic thrillers of all time.

0 552 10522 8 £1.50

BELIEVE THIS . . . YOU'LL BELIEVE ANYTHING
by James Hadley Chase

Clay Burden had married his sluttish young wife, Rhoda, because he was tired of being on his own. Val had walked out on him – and if he couldn't have Val, maybe marriage would make him forget her.

Six years later, working in Paradise City, Clay met Val again. Married to the powerful and sinister Henry Vidal, she had changed . . . still beautiful and passionate, still compelling . . . but tense and nervous, driven by odd fears and anxieties . . .

When Clay left his job and joined the Vidal empire, what had begun as a sneaking feeling of unease hardened into stone-cold certainty. Val must be released from the hypnotic influence exerted over her by her husband – even if Clay had to murder to set her free . . .

0 552 11468 5 95p